HOLD ME

Lindsay McKenna

Blue Turtle Publishing

Praise for Lindsay McKenna

"A treasure of a book... highly recommended reading that everyone will enjoy and learn from."

—Chief Michael Jaco, US Navy SEAL, retired, on Breaking Point

"Readers will root for this complex heroine, scarred both inside and out, and hope she finds peace with her steadfast and loving hero. Rife with realistic conflict and spiced with danger, this is a worthy page-turner."

—BookPage.com on Taking Fire
March 2015 Top Pick in Romance

"... is fast-paced romantic suspense that renders a beautiful love story, start to finish. McKenna's writing is flawless, and her story line fully absorbing. More, please."

—Annalisa Pesek, Library Journal on Taking Fire

"Ms. McKenna masterfully blends the two different paces to convey a beautiful saga about love, trust, patience and having faith in each other."

—Fresh Fiction on Never Surrender

"Genuine and moving, this romantic story set in the complex world of military ops grabs at the heart."

—RT Book Reviews on Risk Taker

"McKenna does a beautiful job of illustrating difficult topics through the development of well-formed, sympathetic characters."

—Publisher's Weekly (starred review) on Wolf Haven
One of the Best Books of 2014, Publisher's Weekly

"McKenna delivers a story that is raw and heartfelt. The relationship between Kell and Leah is both passionate and tender. Kell is the hero every woman wants, and McKenna employs skill and s empathy to craft a physically and emotionally abused character in Leah. Using tension and steady pacing, McKenna is adept at expressing growing, tender love in the midst of high stakes danger."

—RT Book Reviews on Taking Fire

"Her military background lends authenticity to this outstanding tale, and readers will fall in love with the upstanding hero and his fierce determination to save the woman he loves.

—Publishers Weekly (starred review) on *Never Surrender*
One of the Best Books of 2014, Publisher's Weekly

"Readers will find this addition to the Shadow Warriors series full of intensity and action-packed romance. There is great chemistry between the characters and tremendous realism, making Breaking Point a great read."

—RT Book Reviews

"This sequel to Risk Taker is an action-packed, compelling story, and the sizzling chemistry between Ethan and Sarah makes this a good read."

—RT Book Reviews on *Degree of Risk*

"McKenna elicits tears, laughter, fist-pumping triumph, and most all, a desire for the next tale in this powerful series."

—Publishers Weekly (starred review) on *Running Fire*

"McKenna's military experience shines through in this moving tale . . . McKenna (High Country Rebel) skillfully takes readers on an emotional journey into modern warfare and two people's hearts."

—Publisher's Weekly on *Down Range*

"Lindsay McKenna has proven that she knows what she's doing when it comes to these military action/romance books."

—Terry Lynn, Amazon on *Zone of Fire.*

"At no time do you want to put your book down and come back to it later! Last Chance is a well written, fast paced, short (remember that) story that will please any military romance reader!"

—LBDDiaries, Amazon on *Last Chance.*

Risk Taker
Degree of Risk
Breaking Point
Never Surrender
Zone of Fire
Taking Fire
On Fire
Running Fire

THE WYOMING SERIES

Shadows From The Past
Deadly Identity
Deadly Silence
The Last Cowboy
The Wrangler
The Defender
The Loner
High Country Rebel
Wolf Haven
Night Hawk
Out Rider

WIND RIVER VALLEY SERIES, Kensington

2016
Wind River Wrangler

2017
Wind River Rancher
Wind River Cowboy

Dear Reader,

Welcome to the Delos Series and thank you for purchasing this book! I truly hope you enjoy it. If it leaves you with warm fuzzies, please think about writing a review on it for me? Reviews are VERY important and helpful in bringing new readers to my series. If you would love to review but never have, just get a hold of me at my contact information, which can be found at my website lindsaymckenna.com and I'll send you my little article on how to write a dynamite review!

The novella, *Hold Me*, is a continuation of *Hold On* with our hero and heroine Beau and Callie.

Beau Gardner, Army Delta Force sergeant, has only a few months left before he can leave military life behind to marry Callie McKinley, the woman of his dreams. Callie has been recovering from an attack at the hands of the Taliban at her parents' Montana ranch, but she knows Beau must return to Afghanistan. But it is a dangerous place, and Beau soon finds himself in the line of fire.

Let me hear from you about the Delos series. Happy reading!

Dedication

To Tricia Speed, who does it all and I couldn't do it without her!

CHAPTER 1

January 2

CALLIE MCKINLEY TRIED to stuff down her fears as she stood with her fiancé, Beau Gardner, a Delta Force Army sergeant, at the Butte, Montana airport. He was leaving on this cold January under clear skies, typical of a Montana winter morning. She felt his arm curved around her shoulders and took comfort in it, but it didn't dissolve her growing terror as he prepared to complete his fifth tour in Afghanistan. Callie felt his fingers move soothingly up and down her upper arm as she leaned against his tall, hard body. Was he reading her mind? She tried to appear relaxed and calm, but inside she was drowning in a storm of anxiety.

People were making their way home from the Christmas and New Year holidays. Beau was dressed in civilian clothes and Callie didn't think anyone in the bustling airport would know he was a deadly operator. He had saved her life late November when her civilian charity van was attacked by Taliban on the way to a "safe" Afghan village to render medical aid. She had been a devoted child care worker for Hope Charity, spending six months of every year in Kabul, the capital, where she assisted fifty orphaned Afghan babies and young children. She loved her work with them, even while knowing that Kabul wasn't truly safe.

She sighed, resting her brow against Beau's Levi's jacket, closing her eyes and squeezing him around his trim waist. Instantly, Beau responded, dropping a light kiss on her hair and holding her a bit more tightly for a moment, as if to reassure her. He knew she was worried about his going back over there. His enlistment wasn't up until June of this year and it was only January. *Six months*. Callie knew that in the winter, the Taliban attacks slowed down or stopped because the heavy snowfall didn't allow the enemy to travel around the country very easily. They all headed back to Pakistan to wait until the spring thaw in April. Then, they would return to begin systematic attacks against anyone, Afghan, American, or otherwise, who did not share their beliefs.

"You doing okay?" Beau asked as he leaned down, his lips brushing the curve of her ear.

"I'm doing okay," she lied. The last thing

Callie wanted was to have Beau worry about her and not focus on his job in black ops. She heard a rumble in his broad chest.

"You're such a beautiful liar, Ms. McKinley, but I love you anyway."

She absorbed his West Virginia drawl, soothed by the low, husky sound of his voice and feeling how much he loved her. Callie had thought she knew what love was after dating a series of "Mr. Wrongs." Then, Beau, a twenty-seven-year-old Army Delta Force sergeant, had more or less crashed into her life when she was working in Kabul, changing it forever. Rousing herself, she lifted her head, angling it so she could meet his amused gray eyes focused solely on her. Lips twisting, she whispered, "I'm not lying, Beau. Well, maybe a little . . ."

"Hey, I know you. You're a first-class worry wart, sweetheart. I'll be fine," he promised, dropping another kiss on her furrowed brow. "I'll be home before you know it and I'll meet you right here in this airport." He lifted his head, angling his chin. "And Grandpa Graham will be here with you."

Callie rallied a small smile. Her Grandpa Graham, formerly a Marine Corps sniper and black ops veteran, was standing near the swinging doors, looking around as he always did. She supposed it was his top secret security background that made him more alert to the situations around him. "Yes, Grandpa will be here with me, for sure. But the rest of the McKinley family will probably be here to meet you, too. Everyone loves you. You know that." And her Montana ranch family truly did love Beau. He fit in so well with the ranching lifestyle.

His own folks, Cletus and Amber Gardner, lived on Black Mountain in West Virginia. They were from a long line of hill people who had lived over a hundred years on that mountain. Beau might not have come from a ranch background, but he was used to living close to nature, had a rural soul, was a hunter and fisherman, and helped his father, a furniture maker.

"Yes, I love your family," he agreed, rocking her in his arms, squeezing her once more to comfort her. "I can hardly wait for you to meet *my* family. They're dying to meet you."

"Ugh, don't use the word, 'dying,' Beau," she said, wrinkling her nose.

"Oh . . . sorry . . . well, yes, they want to meet the woman I'm going to marry after I get home in June. The good news is that they're driving up here to be with us when we get married at the Eagle Feather Ranch. It's going to be a great big shindig, for sure," he said, smiling down into her eyes.

Beau's love settled over Callie like a warm blanket. She felt it in his gaze, in the way he was holding her against him, rocking her just a little, as if he were rocking a frightened child. And right now, that was exactly how Callie felt. No matter how much she tried to tell herself Beau was going to be all right once he returned to Bagram and conducted his winter missions, her heart was awash in fear. Her emotions were raw, anyway, because she'd gotten a good dose of PTSD from that ambush late last year in Afghanistan.

"I can hardly wait," she whispered shakily.

"Hey, look at it this way. We're going to get married in late June after I return, and we can talk about all the wedding plans before then via Skype and email. There's lots to look forward to doing together in the months ahead, Callie."

Right now, thinking about finding a dress or anything else was the last thing on her mind, but she wanted Beau to think that it was the right answer for now. "You're right. But you can't see the wedding dress until I walk down the aisle with you." She melted beneath his boyish smile, his eyes alight with mischief.

"Ohhh, come on, Callie, I'm black ops. We're pretty good at tracking down wedding dresses!" he chuckled.

She laughed, fighting back tears. Since their escape from the Taliban ambush and during those horrific days and nights on the run, Callie had changed—she was now a fearful, high-strung person. Grandpa Graham assured her it was PTSD and that with time, her anxieties would begin to diminish. But they hadn't. Or maybe she was still too close to the experience and expecting too much, too soon. Beau had been wounded in the attack. His captain allowed him to take leave to see her close to Christmas. He'd arrived here from Afghanistan just before the holiday, and a lot of her PTSD symptoms had gone away. He, too, had PTSD, but had learned to live with it.

Beau had always teased her that having sex was the best way to release the feel-good endorphins that would overwhelm the high cortisol creating her 24/7 anxiety. He was right about that! Even now, her body glowed from their lovemaking before their departure from the ranch.

"I know you would, Beau. Still, I'd like it to be a nice surprise for you."

"Okay," he said in his drawl, "I don't want to disappoint the woman I'm going to marry. I'll be good and not peek, okay? But let's talk about all the other angles of bringing this shindig together, okay?"

Nuzzling her cheek against Beau's chest, closing her eyes and inhaling his male scent, she whispered, "Yes, I'll do that with you." How much she was going to miss him! In her present broken state, she was a hot mess. On the other hand, he was stable, reliable, and in love with her. Having Beau made up for what she'd lost during that ambush and the nearly forty-mile run back to

Bagram. He was like emotional glue, filling her fractured soul, holding her together so she could stabilize.

Callie wondered if she could make it without him—and was aware that these thoughts reflected a major change in her. After all, she was a rancher's daughter, raised in a natural world where being tough in every way was important. She'd been confident, strong, and in love with life until that damned attack.

As if sensing her anxiety, Beau wrapped his arms around her, holding her tightly, resting his cheek against her hair.

"It's going to be okay, Callie. I promise you, I'll be fine. I'm going to go work with Maggie over at the Hope Charity Orphanage on my days off." He laughed a little. "I'll go over there and change babies' diapers and clean out the diaper pail like I did when we met there. Those four Afghan widows and Maggie will love having me around again."

Laughing, burying her head beneath his and hearing the slow pounding of his heart soothed her. She said, "Oh, I already emailed Maggie and told her you'd be dropping by to help her and the orphans when you could. She's tickled pink, Beau." That was where Callie had fallen in love with Beau when he took up security duty at the orphanage with his Delta Force team leader, Sergeant Matt Culver. Her sister, Dara, was a pediatrician, and had also been there helping with the fifty babies and young children. Matt had fallen in love with Dara, she thought, from the moment he saw her at the Thanksgiving USO show at Bagram. Beau swore he'd fallen in love with Callie at the same time because she and Dara had performed a dual belly dancing routine for four thousand servicemen to lift their spirits during the holiday season.

"Yep, I'll become her official diaper changer when I go there to help out," he agreed, grinning widely.

Her face fell as Callie heard the dreaded boarding call for Beau's commercial flight to Seattle, Washington. Her arms automatically tightened around his waist. Scrunching her eyes shut, she wanted to dissolve into his body and always be with him, her love and need for him was so powerful. She felt Beau draw in a slow, ragged breath.

"I gotta go, sweetheart," he rasped, kissing her hair and kissing her cheek. "I love you. I'll be fine, so don't worry. Okay?"

She felt as if she were being torn into bleeding, painful pieces. Releasing him, Callie choked back a sob, her throat tightening. Stepping away from him, lifting her lashes to his narrowing gray gaze, his hands on her upper arms, she whispered, "Don't you *dare* die on me, Beau Gardner, or I'll kill you."

He laughed and shook his head. "You're too funny, Ms. McKinley." His smile disappeared. "I'm going over to tell your grandpa goodbye and I'll be right back."

Nodding, Callie knew her grandpa was deliberately standing apart from them to give them these last few minutes of privacy together. "Yes. He loves you so much, Beau . . ."

She watched Beau nod, smile, and stride over to him. The two men shook hands and she could tell by their body language that there was genuine affection between them. Grandpa Graham had been an unsung hero in the Persian Gulf War. No one would ever know how many men's lives he'd saved that fateful day in Iraq. He and Beau had just naturally gravitated to one another and Callie knew her grandpa treated Beau like the son he'd never had. Beau was special in that way. His easygoing West Virginia charm, his earnestness, and sincere warmth, had made her entire family fall in love with him.

Tears burned in her eyes but Callie swore she wouldn't cry. It would tear Beau apart, and she wanted him to leave thinking she'd be fine. She would cry tonight, alone, without him at her side in their small cabin behind the main ranch house.

The two men hugged one another, slapping each other on the back, and then separated. Callie pasted on a smile, swearing silently to make this parting good for Beau. She didn't want him anxious about her in any way because it could distract him when on a mission and get him killed.

Walking toward him, she smiled up into his eyes, opening her arms. Beau halted and swept her into his arms, his mouth crushing hers. She moaned as he took her lips hungrily and then grew tender, worshipping her, sharing his love for her in another way. Unable to get enough of him, of his strong mouth cherishing hers, she wanted to scream, to cry, to beg him not to get on that plane.

Beau regretfully eased from her soft lips, holding her gaze. "When I get to Bagram I'll email you first thing so you know I arrived safe and sound."

Giving a jerky nod, she said, "Yes, thanks. Just be careful Beau."

He released her and picked up his carry-on bag. "I'm going to marry the girl of my dreams." He leaned over, giving her one last hard, swift kiss on the mouth. "I'll come home to you, sweetheart. That's a promise . . ."

And he was gone.

Just like that.

Callie stood there, watching him disappear down the corridor, heading to the plane. Wrapping her arms around herself, she felt devastated by Beau's immediate absence, even though she could still see him. She knew that he felt the same way, though he didn't show it the way she did.

"Hey," Grandpa Graham whispered, walking up to her, sliding his arm around her hunched shoulders, drawing her against him. "He's going to be all right, baby girl."

Just her grandpa's roughened, low words, soothed some of her terror. "I'm sick with worry," she sobbed, placing her fingers against her lips, looking up into his somber blue gaze. He was a big man at six-feet, five-inches tall, and his once black hair was threaded with silver, still cut military short.

He eased his rough, calloused hand across her mussed red hair. "I know you are. But that's because you love him so much." He patted her arm. "You were brave for him just now, baby girl. I'm proud of you."

Hot tears welled in her eyes and now she sobbed, pressing her hand against her mouth to try and stifle the sounds.

"Let it go, now. You don't have to be brave for Beau anymore," Graham told her roughly, pulling her into his arms and holding her. "Just let it go . . ."

BEAU WAS BLEARY-EYED as he arrived at the Delta Force barracks at Bagram. There were only thirty operators on the team and many of them were home on leave because of the holidays. His room was a sharp contrast to the cozy ranch house he'd left behind. It was plywood with thin walls and he could hear his brother operators snoring in the early morning hours. Throwing his duffle bag on his bunk, he looked at his watch, seeing it was 0400. He'd already checked in with the duty officer, gotten all the paperwork out of the way, and trudged back to his new digs.

The flights were hideous this time of year, filled with uncomfortable passengers packed into too-small seats. He'd slept as much as he could during that time. He breathed in Callie's scent on his Levi's jacket as he shrugged out of it. For a moment, he held it up to his face, inhaling her sweet scent. He'd already sent her an email from the main HQ to let her know he arrived safely. That would give her some peace, at least.

It was snowing right now, not hard, but just enough to make driving around Bagram miserable. Ice on the asphalt had turned it into a skating rink. At this time of year, Beau knew Bagram was pretty much shut down for the holidays, since most people knew the Taliban were back in Pakistan for the winter. He got undressed, found his towel, washcloth, and soap, and padded down the hall to the showers. Everyone else was still fast asleep.

His mind was disoriented from jetlag, coupled with fatigue, but his heart already ached for

Callie's presence. He worried about her because she was still entrenched in the PTSD from what she'd experienced last November. Beau had known she was traumatized from her capture by the Taliban. His captain let him take leave after the attack, close to Christmas, so that he could be with her at that time. Because he'd sustained a gunshot wound to his calf during her rescue, he'd received permission. They had needed each other so much, and their time together had strengthened them both.

As he opened the door to the white tiled area, he placed his towel on a wooden bench outside the five showers. Turning on the faucet, he felt the warm spray of water begin to dissolve some of his jetlag. He lifted his face, allowing the water to drench his black hair. He'd had it cut and trimmed, his beard gone, for going home to Butte to visit Callie. Now it would all grow back. The operators wore beards in order to fit into the male Muslim culture. He wiped his face, the warm water feeling good, washing away the human grit collected during the long, boring flight.

He knew Graham McKinley would take good care of Callie in his absence. The retired Marine sniper would be a fierce guardian for his granddaughter. The men had talked in private about Callie's emotional instability and PTSD. Beau agreed with Graham that she would do much better being outside, riding, working in the barn, and just focusing on keeping busy. He knew that Callie didn't do well in an office setting.

Graham promised him he'd keep Callie outdoors on good days when a blizzard wasn't visiting the area. He loved both his granddaughters, Dara and Callie, but Beau could see that headstrong, wild child Callie, was his personal favorite. Graham would never admit that, but Beau sensed it and his intuition was never wrong about such things. He'd managed to stay alive, thanks to his hunches.

His mind turned to his own parents, Cletus and Amber. They, too, worried about him returning to Afghanistan. Beau knew that there wasn't a time that they weren't worried about their three sons. Coy and Jackson were younger, and they were Marine Recons, black ops. Both were in harm's way all the time, just as he was as a Delta Force operator.

His parents, he knew, tried not to let their worry about their sons overwhelm them. But Beau always tried to put himself in their shoes having three sons in danger all the time. He was seeing it play out personally with Callie, trying her best to put on a brave face so he wouldn't worry about her while he was here in Afghanistan. He knew that there was very little he could do to help her from here, and hoped Graham would take her under his wing and get her through this lonely period.

He scrubbed his hair clean with Afghan lye soap, the only soap he'd use. The Taliban had good noses, and if the wind was right, they would smell the scent and think nothing of it. But if he stupidly brought some U.S. brand of soap and used it on his body, it could be his death knell. The Taliban would smell it and know in a heartbeat that he was the enemy.

His mind moved forward to June, when his enlistment was up and he'd be leaving the Army for good. Never had he envisioned that happening until he'd seen Callie belly dance. At that moment, his whole world had been upended in the most wonderful way. Yes, he'd chased her and proven to her that he wanted a real relationship, not just a roll in the sack, as she'd automatically thought. He couldn't blame her for feeling that way because she was young, vibrant, and beautiful. She easily drew men's attention precisely because of that. When he'd met her, she had been sick and tired of being stalked for sex without love or a commitment.

He smiled through the suds on his face, knowing he had the patience and resolve for the long haul with Callie. She hadn't believed he was sincerely smitten with her at first. He had been a security detail for the Hope Charity Orphanage and had been changing babies' diapers and washing out the diaper buckets for the four Afghan widows who worked there. When she saw him working the diaper brigade, Callie recognized that he was indeed different from the sex-hungry males she had encountered before Beau. From that moment on, she slowly let down her walls and allowed him access to her beautiful, generous heart and body. He'd already fallen in love with her that first night she belly-danced for the Thanksgiving USO show. God, he missed his woman. And it was far more than just missing her sexually. She had captured his heart and soul, too. He wanted no one else in his life but Callie.

Pushing his face beneath the spray of water, eyes closed, he allowed himself to feel his loneliness without Callie at his side. She was a bright sunbeam in everyone's life. Or at least, she had been until that damned Taliban ambush. He and Callie had escaped with her sister, Dara and Matt Culver. The couples had split up in hopes of splitting their Taliban attackers, improving their chances of making it out of that ambush alive. Fortunately, they had all reunited in safety, but the whole nightmare had turned Callie's life inside out.

Turning off the faucet, Beau shook his head, water droplets flying around him. He grabbed the towel sitting on the bench near the entrance. As he padded barefoot out of the shower room, his worry centered on Callie's PTSD. When he'd been with her it had diminished a bit, and he'd talked to Graham about it, who was no stranger to PTSD, either. Callie doted on her grandparents and Beau knew if anyone could steady her in his absence, it would be Graham. She was at a turning point with the symptoms and he hated to leave her in such a vulnerable state.

Rubbing his face and hair dry, he walked to the wall of lockers and dried himself off. At this hour, no one was in the shower area and he was glad because he didn't feel like reconnecting into the dangers of his job just yet.

Before meeting and falling in love with Callie, the Army had been his mistress and he felt complete and satisfied with his lot in life. But once Callie came on stage in that purple belly dancing outfit, the silver coins beneath her breasts and around her hips tinkling and swaying, his moorings with the Army had been torn loose. Suddenly, Beau wanted more, much more. He dreamed of marriage, a partner, and becoming a parent.

His mother, Amber, ever the wise woman, had shaken her calloused finger at him one day when he'd been living at home. He was helping her weed her garden and she told him that someday, he'd meet the woman he was going to marry. And when he did, she'd turn his world topsy-turvy. "Just like that," she predicted, and she'd snapped her fingers, grinning at him from another row of onions she was weeding.

"Ma, that's never gonna happen," he said, chuckling, squatting between two rows of stringed beans.

Amber laughed. "You're too young and you don't know life yet, Beau," she said, smiling over at him. "Your pa saw me when we were just kids, maybe six or seven-years-old, at the Thorn cabin. He says he fell in love with me then."

"How can a six-year-old know he's in love?" Beau scoffed, shaking his head.

"He knew," Amber intoned. She always wore coveralls, the knees blackened with soil. Pushing her wide-brimmed straw hat up off her sweaty brow, she said pertly, "He knew and so did I."

"But did you ever talk about it?"

"Never. We were too young to know what we were feeling, what was pulling us like North and South Pole magnets toward one another."

"You married him when you were eighteen," Beau said.

"Indeed I did. He was nineteen at the time. He'd already gone into his father's furniture making business and was pulling in a right steady income for a hill boy that young. He brought the dowry to my folks and told them he wanted to marry me when I graduated from high school. They said yes."

"But didn't my grandparents talk to you first?" Beau asked, alarmed, sitting up, resting his dirty hands on the thighs of his jeans.

"Of course, but everyone on Black Mountain knew we'd eventually get hitched."

Smiling, Beau went down on all fours, hunting for those pesky weeds. He often helped his mother, as did his younger brothers, Coy and Jackson, with the five-acre garden. "Oh, that's good. But I'm twenty-four, Ma. Not six. I've never met a woman yet that cold cocked me like Pa did you."

Throwing a bunch of weeds into her nearby, white five-gallon plastic bucket, Amber snickered. "You have the magnet gene, as Pa and I call it. When the *right* woman prances in front of you, you'll go down like a felled ox, too, smarty pants." She gave Beau a warm look, her mouth wide with a knowing smile.

He snickered. "Okay, Ma, I believe you. But I just don't think it's gonna happen to me. Maybe to Coy or Jackson. But not to me."

"Just wait and see," she said, waving her finger toward him. "I'm going to die laughing when it does because your head will be in the clouds and you'll be completely flummoxed. Mark my words, young man."

As he dressed in a dark green Army t-shirt and trousers, Beau smiled as he recalled that moment with his mother. Her words had come true. *In spades.* He closed the locker and took his damp towel to a canvas container and dropped it inside. When he checked his watch, he saw that nearly an hour had passed. He calculated that he was ten hours and thirty minutes ahead of Butte, Montana. And it was still Sunday there, right around family dinnertime at five-thirty Mountain Standard Time. They'd all be sitting down for a feast at the long trestle table in the warm, ranch house kitchen.

Beau had loved Sundays with the McKinley clan. His own family was like that, too. Everyone always looked forward to a late afternoon dinner on Sundays.

Only this time, he wasn't seated next to Callie. Graham and his wife, Maisy, would be at either end of the table, with Callie's parents, Connor and Stacy, sitting across from her and Beau. Rubbing his chest, he walked out of the shower area, making sure the door didn't slam shut. Thanks to the plywood rooms, he could hear everything, since there were no real walls or insulation to stop noise. Padding silently down the corridor, he pushed open the door to his tiny, cramped room. It was about as wide as a boxcar and one-third the length. Beau didn't mind. He and his brothers had slept in a small bedroom in their cabin, all squished together in one little room. For him, small, tight spaces were associated with comfort, warmth, and good memories of growing up.

He desperately needed to sleep. His bunk

was high and narrow, with six green wool blankets placed across it. The place was barely above freezing, since the walls weren't insulated and most of the warm air leaked out here and there. The quarters been thrown together by early Delta operators, not wanting to wait for the Navy Seabees to get to them. They already had a long, busy schedule for building accommodations for the various military groups in the area.

Lying down and drawing the thick, heavy blankets over himself, Beau settled back on the goose-down pillow he'd brought from home, and decided that tomorrow he'd Skype Callie to see how she was doing. There was usually at least a twenty-minute wait between Skype calls to family by the operators. But with so many of them gone back to the States for the holidays, Beau knew he wouldn't have to sign up on a list and wait hours for his turn.

He had grown so used to sleeping with Callie and he acutely missed her soft, curved warmth against his body. He also missed her slender, graceful arms and those beautiful, artistic fingers of hers curving around his naked waist. He always looked forward to sleeping with her close to him, her curly red hair tickling his jaw, her cheek against his warm, hard shoulder. After thirty days together, he realized how much he'd lost by not being in love until he was twenty-seven. When he told his mother that he'd fallen in love with Callie, she'd laughed knowingly. And Beau was enough of a gentleman to admit to her that she'd been dead right: Callie McKinley owned him body, heart, and soul.

CHAPTER 2

January 5

C ALLIE ABOUT JUMPED out of her skin when her computer beeped and a Skype message popped up on the screen. Her heart pounded as she hurried to sit down in the small office off the main hallway. It was a little past ten on Monday morning. Was it Beau?

Her hand trembled as she took the mouse and moved it to open up Skype on her screen. Beau's stubbled face appeared and she could see that he was exhausted. She calculated it was around eleven p.m. Tuesday, local Bagram time. He was wearing an old, frayed Army baseball cap and a green t-shirt showing off his impressive chest and broad shoulders. His eyes were bloodshot and he was fatigued. Jetlag, for sure.

"I was so hoping you'd Skype me," she said breathlessly, smiling at him. Now, Callie wished she hadn't put her long, red hair into two braids. She should have left it down because Beau loved running his fingers through its long, thick strands.

"I got lucky," he grinned. "The guy who had this time slot got food poisoning from one of the chow halls, so he offered me his turn. Boy, you're a sight for sore eyes, sweetheart."

Her heart thudded fiercely with love for him. As jetlagged as Beau was, he knew how to lift her sagging spirits. Twining her fingers around one of her braids, she whispered, "I wish I looked prettier for you, maybe with my hair down . . ."

"Shucks, Callie, you're beautiful no matter what you do or don't do with your hair. I didn't fall in love with your hair. I fell in love with *you*."

She knew that all their Skype calls were taped and monitored by the CIA, so she tried to keep their conversation light. "Well, braids make me look like a kid," she said, shrugging, and watched his gray eyes lighten with amusement.

"On the other hand," she teased, "you're looking kinda like a hobo who just missed his train!" She motioned toward his beard.

"Yeah, gotta go back into Muslim mode," he joked, rubbing the side of his bristly face. "What's the weather like where you are?"

"Clear. In fact, the sky is so blue it hurts your eyes to look at this morning, Beau. When I got up earlier, I was staring out the kitchen window wishing you were here. Oh, it would be a great day for a horseback ride on one of those trails." She saw sadness cross his face, but he rallied quickly and said, "Don't I wish . . ." Beau was sitting at the computer monitor, a plywood board for a desk in a small room, the door closed so they could have some modicum of privacy. How she treasured these moments.

"Think June, sweetheart," he urged. "Every day here is a day closer to coming home to you. How are you doing?"

She forced a smile and said, "I'm doing okay, but I miss you a lot." She wanted to add: *terribly*, but bit back on the word. Beau was missing her just as much as she was missing him.

"Good. Has Graham got any plans for you today?"

"Yes," she said, her voice lighter. She grinned, "In fact, we're going out to the tack room in a little while because we've got to clean a lot of leather. With half the wranglers gone for the winter, things like that fall on him to handle." She held up her hand, wriggling her fingers. "He asked if I wanted to help and I said I would. It makes no sense for him to do all those saddles, bridles, and martingales alone."

"How warm will it be in there? I know that tack room isn't heated."

"Probably above freezing. He went out earlier and put a big heater in there to start warming it up, so it ought to be fine. My mom is making a big pot of vegetable beef soup for lunch and dinner, and my grandma is in the kitchen making six loaves of bread. I think by the time I get done cleaning leather at noon, I'll be more than ready to eat."

"Good. At least at your place, no one gets food poisoning! I really wish I was there with you," he said, smiling a little.

Callie could feel him wanting to say so much more, but black ops had top secret clearances and the CIA wanted to make sure they didn't slip up and give away classified intel. "I wish I could pack up some of my mom's soup, put it in dry ice, and send it to you."

"Wish you could, too, but it would never work."

"Grandma Maisy was talking about maybe tomorrow having me come into the kitchen and help make up about ten dozen chocolate chip cookies and send them to you. That way you could share them with your brothers." She saw Beau perk up, since he loved desserts.

"That would be right nice. We've only got about half our teams here. The rest are stateside until February one. Wrap the cookies well, and I'm sure everyone will get at least two."

"Sounds good. I'll tell Grams." She gave him a wicked look. "And of course, you can stash a few away for yourself in your room, can't you,

Gardner?"

He nodded. "Caught!" he grinned, and his cheeks flushed. He could be so boyish when he was alone with her and she loved that he'd let himself be vulnerable with her. That was the man she fell in love with.

"Well, I'd be tellin' a big fib if I didn't agree that I'd probably take a dozen and parcel 'em out for myself, one cookie a day. That way, when I eat it, I'll close my eyes, visualize the ranch, and see you beside me."

Her heart turned over. "I'd love that," she said. And then, speaking more softly, she whispered, "I miss you so much, Beau."

"I know you do. I miss you just as much, believe me. But we'll get through this. We have our whole lives ahead of us. Speaking of which, have you and Maisy and Stacy had a chance to go into Butte, to the wedding shops? Did you look at any wedding gowns, yet?"

"We'll probably go this Saturday. Grams made an appointment at one shop at ten in the morning. We're all looking forward to having some girl fun on our visit there."

"Girl fun is good for you," he agreed amiably.

"My grandpa and dad will be watching the Saturday college football games while we're shopping in Butte."

He rubbed his hands. "Now, you're really

making me jealous! I'd like to be right there in that big living room watching with 'em."

Laughing, Callie said, "Yes, you sure would be right there with them. Hey, on another topic? Grandpa said he's working on some blueprints for an addition to our little cabin out back. I'm going to find some way to email them as a zip file to you so you can look at them. He'd love your feedback."

"Great. He and I talked a lot about the size of the rooms and where they'd be before I left."

"I know." She sighed. "My Grandpa loves you so much, Beau. He's had nothing but girls surrounding him, and now you're the only boy in the family. He feels like you're his long-awaited grandson."

"We sure get along well," he agreed, looking pleased. He looked at the watch on his wrist. "Uh, oh! Looks like my twenty minutes are up, sweetheart, so I gotta go. Things are quiet around here. Tomorrow's my first day at Hope Charity doing security rounds and baby diapering." He grinned. "Maggie's jumping with joy that I've come back to help."

"I wish I were there with you," she said, frowning. "But my PTSD is still too raw."

"But it's quieting down a little?"

Callie felt Beau's concern. She waved her hands. "I'm doing fine. I'm sleeping like a baby, and much of that is thanks to Grandpa! He has me working outside every day we don't have snow. With all that physical exercise and fresh air, I have less anxiety. Hey, don't worry about me, Beau. I'm fine."

February 14

"HEY, CALLIE," STACY called down the hall of the main ranch house, "there's someone here to see you."

Callie poked her head out of the kitchen where she was making another batch of cookies to send over to Beau and the guys at Bagram. "Who?" Callie asked, puzzled. She wasn't expecting anyone.

Her mother's green eyes shone with mirth. At forty-five, she was vibrant and a picture of health. She kept busy balancing the accounting books for the ranch, and could usually be found in her small office keeping up with expenses.

Now, she stood at the half-opened door. "Come here," she beckoned mysteriously."

Intrigued, Callie wiped her hands on her apron and walked down the hall to see what was making her mother smile. "What's going on?" she demanded, seeing a sly look in her mother's face.

"Come see," she urged, stepping aside.

Callie opened the front door, her eyes widening. It was the FTD florist from Butte, and the delivery man was holding two parcels in his hands.

"Ma'am, are you Ms. Callie McKinley?" he asked.

"Well . . . yes." She saw the young man smile. He had a long box under one arm and another box beneath it.

"These are for you, Ma'am. Would you like to take them? I need you to sign for them."

Frowning, she said, "Well, yes, but who are they from?"

"A Mr. Beau Gardner."

Gasping, Callie heard her mother chuckle and come up, sliding her arm around her shoulders. Callie gave her a look. "You knew?"

"Well," Stacy admitted coyly, touching her blond ponytail, "Sort of . . . go ahead, get your flowers and gift."

Callie opened the screen door. Stacy helped her bring in the two boxes, setting them on the family's hundred-year-old mahogany table. She signed for the delivery and thanked the young FTD driver. He tipped his hat and then hurried down the walkway her grandpa had cleared of snow earlier that morning. The winter sky was heavy and dark, promising another blizzard in the area in about twelve hours.

Shutting the door, she looked at the gift. "Beau sent these?"

"Well," Stacy said, picking up the box containing the flowers, "let's open them in the kitchen and find out. I'll call Graham and Maisy to come join us."

Callie picked up a large box that weighed at least three pounds and followed her mother into the kitchen. The women placed the boxes on the trestle table. "Tell me more, Mom. Did Beau really send these to me?"

"Well, honey, he emailed Grandpa and asked him to get you flowers and chocolates for Valentine's Day. Want to open them up?"

Touched to the point of tears, Callie opened the flower box. A dozen red roses wrapped in a gold ribbon stared back at her. Gasping, she eased them out of the box that also held a pink translucent vase. "Oh," she whispered, her voice shaky, "these are beautiful, Mom. They smell so good!"

At that moment, Graham and Maisy entered the kitchen, all smiles.

"Look, aren't these beautiful?" Callie asked, lifting her head.

"Sure are, baby girl," Graham said, grinning broadly.

Maisy leaned over, smelling the roses, keeping her red hair now sprinkled with silver, to one side. "Oh, what a wonderful fragrance, Callie. They'll fill your cabin with it."

"Open the other box," Graham suggested, gesturing toward it.

"I'll put the roses in the vase," Stacy said taking them from her daughter.

"Thanks, Mom." Callie gave her grandparents a wicked look. "You two were in cahoots with Beau on this plan, weren't you?"

Graham rocked back on the heels of his cowboy boots, hands stuck in the pockets of his Levi's. His gray eyes were filled with mirth. "Oh, just a little." He gave Maisy a warm look of congratulations. "Actually, Maisy is the one who went to the florist in town, but I'm the one who ordered what Beau told me to, since he couldn't be here." He nodded toward the unopened box sitting on the table.

Laughing, Callie hugged her grandparents. "You're such sly foxes!"

"Open it up," Graham urged mildly.

Callie did, and gasped. Inside was a huge, three-pound, heart-shaped box of chocolates. Pulling it out, she said, "This is a *lot* of candy, Grandpa."

"We figured," Stacy said, bringing the roses back in the pink vase, "you might share a few pieces with all of us?"

Laughing with them, she nodded. "If I ate them all myself, I wouldn't fit into my wedding dress!"

"Well," Maisy said, tapping her shoulder, "Beau said we're supposed to get you to eat more. You're still underweight, Callie. He wanted a nice, big box for you."

Warmed by their caring, she opened the box of chocolates. There were truffles, others filled with nuts, some with fruit, and some caramels. "Oh, boy," Callie laughed. "If Beau was here, he'd be gobbling these up, big time."

Graham chortled. "Yeah, you'd have to hide them from that boy. He's got quite a sweet tooth."

"Yes," Stacy said, smiling, "but he's black ops. He'd find where Callie hid them and eat them anyway."

"That's the truth!" Maisy laughed.

"Here's a card," Stacy said, finding it hidden beneath the tissue in the flower box. She grinned as she handed it to Callie.

"Now, Callie," her grandfather said, becoming serious, "that card *is* from Beau. He sent it ahead of time, and Maisy drove in to town the other day so it would be with the flowers in the box."

The thick white parchment envelope tingled in Callie's fingertips. "Oh, this is such a wonderful surprise," she choked, giving them all a look of thanks.

"This boy really loves you," Graham said. "He's a stellar guy in our book, baby girl."

Holding back tears, she said, "Thanks so much, to all of you," and reached out to hug her mother and grandparents.

Maisy slid her arm around Callie's waist. "Tell you what, how about if Grandpa takes these beautiful roses to your cabin while it's still warm outside? You can go to the living room and open up that card and read it privately."

Callie hugged her grandmother, who was almost exactly her height. Maisy always wore jeans and a warm sweater during the wintertime. She didn't look her age of sixty-two, thanks to the physically active life she led on the ranch.

"Okay, I'll do that." She gave them a merry look. "Why don't you get some Ziploc bags out and take what you want from the box of chocolates?"

"Good idea," Stacy said, heading for a drawer near the sink. "We'll leave you some, though."

"It will be Beau's gift to all of us. He'd like that," Callie said, pressing the envelope to her breast. "I'll be back in a minute," and she hurried down the hall to the huge living room.

Callie sat down on a leather couch near the snapping, popping wood burning in the fireplace. Her fingers trembled as she held the envelope on her lap, feeling so much emotion flowing through her. She hoped this would be the last time they would be apart on this special holiday.

Finally opening the envelope, she smiled as the front of the card revealed two people sitting on a wooden bench in front of a calm lake, the glowing sunrise reflected on its glassy surface.

The couple sat close together, the man's arm around his girl's waist. She was leaning her head against his shoulder. At the top, in gold letters, it read, *'To the woman I love . . .'*

She opened up the card. Instead of a verse was a handwritten message from Beau, spanning both sides of the card. In the corner, he'd drawn two hearts with smiling faces on them. She moved her fingertips across his handwritten scrawl, and her lips drew into a smile.

I'm sorry I can't be there to celebrate All Heart's Day with you, Callie. But just know that you are snug in my heart and I'm thinking of you. I miss you so much. My cot feels cold without your warmth, your arms around me. I miss making love with you, hearing those happy sounds you make as I please you. I know this time is especially tough on you. With all my heart I wish I could be the one to knock on that screen door of your parents' ranch home and present you with these red roses and box of chocolates. Your grandparents and parents all had a hand in this sneaky strategy to get you something for Valentine's Day, even though I couldn't be present to give them to you myself.

Just know that I'm picturing us lying together on that bed in our small cabin, my arms around you, kissing you, drowning in your love, your heat, and heart that surrounds me. Let's use this time apart to dream of our life the way we see it happening in the near future. I'm looking forward to those blueprints that Graham is having made of the three new rooms for our cabin. Send me paint chips for those rooms and the colors you'd like to see them painted. Send me jpegs of the type of furniture you'd like see in each room, and maybe even some fabric swatches. Let's use this time to plan for those added on rooms.

I love you, woman of my heart. You fill mine to overflowing. I don't know what I did to deserve someone so beautiful and special as you, but I'm grateful. My life is yours. My heart is yours. And it will be forever. Love, Beau.

Warm tears trickled down her cheeks as she pressed the card to her heart, her eyes closing. Soft sobs tore from her and she pressed her hand against her lips so no one could hear her.

"Baby girl?"

Callie opened her eyes, seeing her grandfather standing in front of her, regarding her tenderly.

"I-I didn't hear you."

One corner of his mouth quirked. "That's probably because I was black ops, too, once upon a time. Could you use some company right now?"

Nodding, she said, "Y-yes . . . sit down, Grandpa," and she patted the couch next to her.

She loved his scent. It was a combination of the cold Montana winter air, the fragrance of the pine trees that encircled half of the home area, and his own, special scent that was only him. His skin was tough, darkened by so many years beneath the sunlight, his hands scarred, calloused, and rough as he sat down and curved his arm around her hunched shoulders.

"Come here," he murmured against her hair, "and just let me hold you for a bit."

It was so easy to lean against her grandfather, feeling the warm strength of his gentle embrace as he held her. She pressed her face into his blue and white flannel shirt, the ache in her heart growing. "I-I miss him so much," she sobbed.

"I know you do, honey. But time is moving along," he said gruffly, patting her shoulder.

"Beau doesn't have anyone to hold him like you're holding me," she sobbed.

"He's strong in different ways from you, Callie, and that's okay. Beau is mature for his age. He's seen a lot. He knows what's important and has a lot of patience. I'm sure he's missing you just as much as you miss him."

"Yesterday was Valentine's Day at Bagram," she sniffed, wiping her eyes.

"And I'm sure he's thinking about you right now. Maybe, when you feel up to it, you can send him an email. I'm sure he'd like to hear from you, about how you liked the red roses and that big box of chocolates. Maybe you can take a few photos of them."

She smiled a little, hearing the amusement in his gruff voice. "You and he are like twins joined at the hip. I swear. You're a big candy eater, too, Grandpa."

Chuckling, he said, "Guilty as charged."

"I did send him an e-card for Valentine's Day but I didn't hear from him. I know he's working at Hope Charity for the next few days because his captain gave him the time off to do it."

"I'm sure when he gets back to base and he sees your card, he'll be over the moon, Callie."

She eased away from him, holding his dark gray gaze. "How did you know?"

"What?"

"That I needed you?"

His mouth compressed. "I've always had a special link with you, baby girl, ever since I held you for the first time shortly after your birth." He eased his arm from around her. "Feel better now?"

"Much," she said, giving him a grateful look. "Thank you."

"Stacy will have lunch ready in an hour. We'll see you then, okay?" He rose.

Lifting her chin, she nodded. "Yes. I'll go home and email Beau. He needs to know how much I love what he wrote to me." She saw Graham place his hands on his hips and give her a pleased look.

"That young man of yours is one in a billion, Callie. And I know his love for you is true and forever."

The word "forever" resonated strongly with her. "I didn't have any idea when I met him how lucky I was, Grandpa. At first, I didn't want anything to do with him because I believed he wanted me only for sex like thousands of other guys at Bagram. I hated how they stalked women like that."

Graham rubbed his strong chin. "He told me that those first couple of days with you were real touch-and-go. But he said that as soon as he started diapering babies, cleaning their bottoms, and washing out the diaper pail, you changed your mind about him," he chuckled.

Rolling her eyes, Callie laughed with him. "That's true. He told me the truth when I asked him why he'd bothered to come to Hope Charity. I knew he was pursuing me, but what surprised me was that he was honest about it. And he was the first guy to ever fess up."

"And he won your heart because of the children he cared for at the orphanage?"

Nodding, she smoothed her hands over the card. "Yes . . . yes, he did, Grandpa." She smiled up at him. "He's so much like you. Mom was telling me that you were changing Dara's and my diapers when we were babies, too."

"Well, he's not a Marine," Graham teased, "but even though he's Army, he has the heart of a Marine." He leaned down, tousling her hair. "And he's coming home to you, baby girl. You're looking better now."

"That's true," she murmured. "Most of all because all of you are here to support me."

"Well, that's what family is for," he said, his voice gravelly with emotion. "We'll see you for lunch, then?"

"I'll be there," she promised. Reaching out, she gripped his work-worn hand, squeezing it. "I just don't know what we'd ever do without you and Grandma." There was a catch in her voice as she saw his gray eyes lighten and she felt his love for her.

"You and Dara will be haunted by us for a long, long time to come," he teased, squeezing her fingers and releasing them.

Callie watched her tall, proud grandfather walk quietly out of the room. She always marveled at his ability to walk without being heard, but Beau had told her one night after they'd made love that being a sniper meant never being seen or heard.

With a sigh, she stood up, gripping the card in her hand, imagining feeling Beau's energy with every word he'd written to her. No longer was she the frightened little girl that he left. The last month and a half had been healing for her. Just getting away from a war-torn country where life and death could happen in the blink of an eye had settled her raw nerves. Now she slept at night. And just as Beau had told her, the nightmares and flashbacks would lessen, and they had. Now, she felt more like the old Callie before the ambush had changed her life forever. Hurrying to the foyer she grabbed her coat, hat, and mittens. She was eager to sit down and write Beau a long, wonderful, super-loving email.

CHAPTER 3

April 2

BEAU WAS MORE focused on danger than usual when he arrived at Hope Charity in busy, downtown Kabul. It was market day, and the whole city was on edge, since this was the day the Taliban frequently planted bombs in various markets around the city.

He stood outside the rear door, watching the foot traffic. Women in black, thick wool burkas with large baskets or sacks in their hands, hurried toward the market two blocks away. He would always remember that while Dara and Callie were here last November at the orphanage, two bombs had gone off in that market. Everyone had been shaken, and the children terrified. Maggie and the four Afghan widows who worked for her had herded all the crying, frightened children into their safe room for protection. Only Matt Culver had been there when it had happened.

Turning his head, Beau scanned the shining, black asphalt highway with its many white Toyota Hilux pickups. The Taliban used them all the time, but so did the everyday residents of Kabul. There was a smattering of taxis bringing some women to the market, too, but most of them walked to it. The sky above was spotted with gray, low-level clouds with occasional glimpses of a blue sky above them. It was early April, and he supposed that this was probably the last snowstorm of the year. The temperature was around forty and he could see the half-inch of snow that had fallen, quickly melting away.

Wearing civilian clothes and a black baseball cap, he leaned against the railing, one heel hooked on a lower rail, the M-4 rifle butt balanced on his thigh. On his gloves, the trigger finger fabric had been cut away so he had physical contact with his weapon. Beau knew that despite his civilian clothing, he'd be spotted as a black ops soldier of some kind by knowing enemy eyes. He was tall, white, male, and bearded. While he'd never pass for an Afghan it was important that he not wear military gear because he'd become the focus of the enemy as soon as he was spotted.

His mind wandered back to his Kevlar vest that he'd left indoors, hanging over the back of Maggie's chair. He hated wearing it unless he had to because it was a level four vest and held heavy ceramic plates in it. His thoughts turned to Callie. Earlier, he'd gotten an email from her before he'd left for work. She told him that the snow was melting quickly in Montana. Now that it was early April, all of the wranglers working for the Eagle Feather Ranch were back. Graham McKinley, owner and foreman, had every one of them out riding the fence line. The heavy, deep Montana snow had taken down weakened wooden posts and they had to be found, replaced, or mended before the wranglers could move on to the next one. Callie said she was riding with one team digging post holes, helping the wranglers with the stringing of new barbed wire.

Smiling a little, his heart warmed. Callie was clearly an outdoors woman and wasn't afraid of hard, physical work. That was one reason why she was such a fantastic belly dancer!

He decided to walk down the few steps to the concrete sidewalk. Everything around him appeared peaceful, but after five tours in Bagram, he knew looks could be deceiving. Beau could feel his gut tighten as the mid-morning sun rose somewhere above the grumpy gray clouds. Once the market opened in a few more minutes, everyone would be on guard. No longer did women, who usually came with children to the market, linger or chat as they used to. Now, they kept their children at home for fear of having them die in a bomb blast.

To maximize their time at the market, the women would rush to certain vendors, hurriedly get their food for the week, and dash out of the area to avoid a possible explosion. He didn't know how long these people could continue to handle it, but if one looked in their eyes, they could see that they were traumatized for life.

Beau walked around the side of the orphanage, between the stucco building and the ten-foot-high wrought iron fence that kept everyone out. Theft was a constant in Kabul, so at the top of the spear-like points of the fence, concertina wire had been strung up by a Delta Force team after the market bombing last November.

Since it had been strung, there had been no more attempts by thieves to break in and steal food, medicine, or money from the orphanage. Hope Charity had so little to begin with and each month was a squeaker as to whether they'd have enough food, enough blankets, or shoes for the children. Maggie was constantly balancing the books.

Beau stopped walking as he picked up the roar of a pickup's engine a block away. His gaze snapped to the highway. Damn! Six men with AK-47s stood in the back of the truck, racing his direction. *Taliban!* Cursing, Beau had no time to call out a warning as the AK-47s barked, and bullets whistled around his head, spatting up mud in front and around him where he stood near the playground within the enclosure. No doubt about it—Beau was their target!

Without thinking, he went down on one knee, taking the safety off his M-4, and jamming it into his right shoulder, sighting the group through the crosshairs. The Taliban were firing at the buildings on either side of the highway, including the orphanage. Grimly, he put his sights on the driver, squeezing off a shot. The wind-shield shattered inward and the truck careened suddenly to the left. Beau watched it flip over, throwing out all six enemy soldiers. They flew through the air like rag dolls, cartwheeling, rifles flying out of their hands, and into the air.

Four of the men slammed into the nearby walls of the unforgiving buildings. They were dead on impact. Beau got up, racing toward the gate. He knew that Maggie had heard the commotion, and he was sure the children were being swiftly gathered up and herded to the safe room within the orphanage. Digging the toes of his boots into the mud, he raced to the locked gate, his M-4 held up and ready to fire at a moment's notice. He worried about shots that might have shattered one of the windows, flying inside, perhaps striking a child or one of the women.

He saw one man in the cab crawl out of the sprung door. Beau fired, killing him with a head shot. Another soldier, who was clearly injured, picked up his rifle while lying on his belly, and fired at Beau.

Beau fired off a simultaneous shot at the lone survivor.

He felt a hot, stinging sensation in his lower ribcage as he was flung backward, off his feet. Slamming into the mud and snow, Beau held onto his M-4. He'd seen his bullet kill the man who had shot at him. The air woofed out of him and he felt suddenly unable to breathe. *What the hell!* Simultaneously, he heard Maggie screaming, her voice growing closer and closer to where he lay on his back, gasping for air.

Maggie dropped to her knees, her eyes wide with terror, reaching out for him.

Beau tried to talk. Instead, blood burbled up and out of his mouth. Stunned, he realized he was wounded. Maggie was crying and telling him to lie still. He tried to get up, but lost consciousness, and then, he remembered nothing more.

April 1, Eagle Feather Ranch, Butte, Montana
THE KNOCKING ON Callie's cabin door pulled her out of a deep sleep. Drowsily, she pushed herself up into a sitting position. Pushing her hair off her face, she squinted at the clock on the dresser opposite the bed: three a.m.

The knocking grew louder and more insistent.

Something was wrong! She slid out of bed, pulling her flannel nightgown downward, the warm, fuzzy fabric falling around her ankles. Quickly pushing her feet into sheepskin slippers, Callie grabbed her chenille robe around herself. What was wrong? Was it one of her grandparents? Her parents?

Swiftly, she jerked open the bedroom door, rushing down the hall to the front door. Outside, she could see the silhouette of a man surrounded in the full moon's light. It was her grandfather! She quickly unlocked the door. His face was shadowed by the lantern style light above the porch. He was dressed in his PJs and a heavy, red wool bathrobe. His eyes were stormy and his mouth thin. Her heart rate took off.

"Grandpa? What's going on? Are you all right?"

"I'm fine. Let me come in, Callie."

"Oh," she mumbled, apologetically, "I'm sorry. Come in," and she stepped aside.

Graham turned and waited until she closed the door. "Come sit with me on the couch, Callie."

Terror raced through her. She stood paralyzed, her gaze locking with his. "It's Beau . . . oh, God . . . what's happened to him?"

Gently, Graham slid his hand around her

arm and led her to the couch. "Come, sit down."

Her knees went weak and Callie dropped to the couch, gripping her suddenly chilled hands, her gaze never leaving his. She'd never seen Graham this serious and it frightened her ten times more. "What's happened to Beau?" she whispered unsteadily.

Graham sat next to her, his hand over hers in her lap. "We just received a call from the Department of Defense notifying us that Beau has been wounded."

Callie gasped. "No!"

His hand tightened around hers. "He's on a flight to Landstuhl Medical Center in Germany, Callie. He sustained a gunshot wound to the lower right side of his ribcage. The docs at Bagram said the lower one third of his right lung is destroyed. He's stable and he's going to live."

Terror turned to relief. Her eyes rounded. "How . . . what happened?"

"I know most of the people at the Department of Defense. Told them who I was and I got more information than they'd normally give out. Beau was at the Hope Charity, making security rounds when a Taliban pickup, six soldiers in the rear with AK-47s, raced down the road, firing at everything and everyone. Beau fired back. He hit the driver and the truck flipped over. It killed all but one man, who fired back at him and hit Beau with a side shot that nicked the lower third of his right lung. Unfortunately, from what the caller said, he's going to lose that part of his lung. However, the bullet went through at such an angle it did not do any damage to his other organs. He was lucky."

Callie was stunned, reeling with all the news. "You said he's going to live, Grandpa. Is that right?"

Nodding, Graham said, "Yes. They've stabilized him and he's already on a C-5 flight to Germany right now. They're prepping him for surgery and once the plane lands, he'll go straight to the medical center to be operated on."

She pulled one hand free, holding it over her pounding heart. "He'll live . . ." That meant more than anything else to her right now. Graham released her other hand, his gruff voice softening a little.

"Yes. I asked the caller for more medical information and they patched me through to the surgeon who's going to perform the surgery on Beau once he arrives. I got special treatment and I'm indebted to them. The surgeon promised to call me directly once Beau is out of surgery and in recovery. Usually, they keep a wounded soldier or Marine for two to three days, and then they're flown here to the States for continuing recovery."

"When is the surgeon going to call you? Did he say how long the surgery would take?"

"He said it depended upon a lot of things. If

there's no compromise to other organs in the area, it's going to be around seven hours."

Pressing her hand to her eyes, she whispered, "Oh, God . . ." Tears leaked between her fingers as she sat there hunched over, her mind spinning, her emotions at hurricane force. "W-what can I do, Grandpa? Can I fly to Germany to be with him?"

He shook his head. "Callie, we'll know more within twelve hours. It would take us twenty-four hours to fly to Germany. And the surgeon said Beau wouldn't be there for more than two days with that type of wound. We'd get there and they'd be taking him out on another C-5 flight heading stateside."

Her stomach fell and she suddenly felt nauseous, relief entwining with future fears and possibilities. "What does it mean to lose part of your lung, Grandpa?"

"Well," he said, holding her tearful gaze, "one thing is for sure. Beau's going to receive a full medical discharge. He needs a complete set of lungs to remain a black ops soldier. He won't have the oxygen levels an operator needs when he's in major distress or running for his life. He'll have less oxygen available to him, Callie, but it won't bother him at all as a civilian. But he's done soldiering, honey."

She wiped her face, her voice wobbly. "That means he's coming home once and for all, doesn't it?"

Nodding, Graham slid his hand across her hunched, taut shoulders, moving it slowly back and forth, trying to get her to relax. "Yes, it means exactly that. And that's good news."

"Where will they take him?"

"Doc said they'll be flying him into Joint Base Andrews outside of Washington, D.C. Then, he'll be transported by ambulance to Walter Reed National Military Medical Center in Bethesda, Maryland. He'll be kept there until he's discharged."

"Can I see him, then?"

Nodding, Graham said, "Just as soon as we know when they're leaving Germany, you and I are going to fly to Maryland. We'll be there to meet him. Okay with you?"

Callie couldn't stem her tears and she sniffed, reaching out, gripping her grandfather's hand. His face was hard, expressionless, but his eyes were bright with emotion. "I-I'd really appreciate that."

"Okay," he said, "I know it's going to be hard for you to sleep the rest of the night. Why don't you get dressed, Callie and I'll wait out here for you. Then, we'll go over to the main ranch house. Grandma is up and making us some hot chocolate. Your parents are up, too. We'll all sit at the kitchen table, have hot chocolate, and wait. I think you should stay over there with us until the surgeon gives me a call, and when he does I'll let you talk to him as well. Okay?"

Right now, Callie needed their support as never before. "Beau's not going to die," she whispered.

"No. He's going to pull through this. Go on, get dressed. You need to be surrounded with family right now."

"But what about Beau's parents? Do they know what happened to him?"

"Yes, they've been informed."

"Could you call them and talk to them? Tell them what else you know?"

He smiled a little. "I was going to do that when we got back to the main house."

She stood up. "Then I need to get moving."

"That's the spirit."

AT TEN A.M., the phone rang sharply in the main ranch house. Callie, already on edge, jumped. The entire family was going about their daily jobs while Callie was nervously knitting, trying to still her trembling fingers, her mind going wild with terror that Beau could die on the surgery table.

Earlier, her grandfather had called Mr. and Mrs. Gardner in Black Mountain, West Virginia. By giving Beau's parents the good news that their son would survive, she could see his tight features soften, knowing he was giving them the best of news.

Graham asked if they could fly to the medical center in Maryland to see him, but they couldn't afford it. But depending upon how long Beau was going to be at Walter Reed, Cletus Gardner said they'd hop in their old pickup truck and drive there to be with their wounded son.

Most heartwarming for Callie was that both wanted to speak to her. That had surprised her, but it shouldn't have because Beau reflected his parents in kindness and thoughtfulness. For the first time since Christmas, when Beau had called and introduced Callie to his parents, they'd talked again.

She saw Graham get up and answer the phone sitting on one of the lampstands near the couch where she sat knitting. Instantly, she stopped knitting as he sat down. Her mother and father walked into the living room, standing, grim looks on their faces. Grandma Maisy came in from the kitchen, her hands dusted with flour from making three blackberry pies for the family this evening. She, too, looked strained and was as exhausted as Callie felt.

Graham was quickly taking notes, grunting every now and then. Once, he turned, winking in her direction. Callie felt her shoulders relax and let the tension bleed out of her. She knew then that Beau had survived the surgery and was all right, but it was so hard to sit and wait. She wanted to grab the phone out of his hand and ask the surgeon a hundred questions, even though she knew her grandfather would ask every question she had in mind.

The call took ten minutes, and then Callie got her turn to talk to Dr. Westover, the surgeon. Afterwards, the doctor said he wanted to speak to Graham again. When they were finished, Graham hung up the phone and the whole family gathered around the couch, that same tension and worry in their expression.

He turned to Callie. "Beau is going to make it."

"Thank God," Callie whispered, her voice cracking.

"That's the best of news!" Maisy said, giving her a warm smile.

Callie saw the anxiety in her parents' faces begin to recede.

"Now," Graham cautioned the family, "the surgeon said they had to remove the lower one-third of Beau's right lung. There was no more damage from the gunshot and that's really good news. He'll be on a flight out of Germany tomorrow morning. He'll arrive at Walter Reed Medical Center and the doc said he'll instruct a nurse on board that flight to text you Beau's information and where he'll be assigned at the medical center. Also, there's a phone at the nurse's station on the floor where he'll be assigned a ward and bed number. He said he knows the doctor assigned to Beau, Major Terry Benson, a pulmonary specialist, a Marine." He grinned slightly. "He's got the best possible doc. He's a Marine and he'll take good care of Beau, no question."

"That's even better news, Grandpa," Callie agreed.

Nodding, Graham said, "When Maisy gets that flour off her fingers, maybe she'll make flight reservations for you and me to go to Maryland. By that time, Beau will be in his ward, settled in, and ready to see visitors. How does that sound?"

Swallowing convulsively, Callie whispered, "That's more than fine, Grandpa . . . thank you . . . so much." She gripped his hand, tears trailing down her face.

"You heard me ask if you could speak to Beau after he's out of recovery and the doc said 'no?' He felt it would be best if you do that when we see him stateside."

Giving a jerky nod, Callie said, "Okay . . . I want so badly to hear his voice, to tell him how much I love him."

"I know," her mother said, giving her daughter a watery smile, "but he's probably barely conscious and in shock with all that's happened to him."

"Not to mention," Maisy added, "that he is

still coming out from under anesthesia and that messes with a person's memory and thought processes. He might not even know you yet, Callie, so I think the surgeon is right about this."

"Will he be conscious at Bethesda?" she asked, looking at her grandfather.

"I'm sure he will be," Graham said. "You just have to be a little more patient for a bit longer."

"Patience is the one thing I'm short on, Grandpa."

He chuckled. "All youngsters your age are like that." He gave his wife, Maisy, a fond look. "We're in our sixties. Patience is something we've learned to practice, haven't we, darlin'."

Maisy smiled, "Indeed." She gave Callie an amused look. "Raising children teaches you patience."

Callie felt lightness in her heart for the first time. Beau was wounded, he had survived surgery and now, he was coming home! Home to her, to his family, to her family. Everyone loved him and she knew everyone was praying for him.

Callie had felt the electric charge that went through the air when the phone rang, and now, it had begun to dissipate. She wondered how Beau was doing. Was he in pain? How badly she wanted to wrap her arms around him and just hold him, tell him how much she loved him.

Two days.

Could she hold herself together for that

long? What made it bearable was that her grandfather was coming along. He'd been in the military and he knew the customs, had good contacts, and could negotiate to get information. And he had that Marine pride and calm centeredness that was always with him, a silent introduction to anyone. She couldn't see anyone telling him 'no.' He would find a way around it.

Beau had told her one night, as he held her in bed, that her grandfather was a man everyone instantly respected because he reflected the best of the military. And people recognized his automatic authority, trusted him, and did what he requested. She hoped he would bring all that to bear so that she could be with Beau in two days. She was on his military record as being his fiancée; therefore, she would be his wife. That was why they had called her first to inform her that he'd been wounded. She was so glad that Beau had put that special paperwork through when he got back to Bagram. Otherwise, she'd not have known he was wounded. Only his family would know. Although, she knew Amber and Cletus Gardner would have instantly called her as soon as they'd found out.

Waiting. She had to wait. She struggled to put her fears away, the PTSD that held her in its grip was awake and pacing through her. Beau had told her that any time there was another crisis in her life, it would return. Well, it had.

CHAPTER 4

BEAU'S HEART LEAPT when he saw Callie enter his hospital ward. He saw her worried expression turn to melting love for him as she hurried down the aisle, beds on either side of the ward. Nurses and other medical personnel flitted back and forth between the wounded Army and Air Force personnel.

His throat tightened, raw from the tube that had been placed inside him for surgery at Landstuhl two days earlier. He was sitting up in Fowler's position, a comfortable angle, to help aid his breathing. He tried to smile but failed, feeling weak from the opiate dripping into one of two IVs that were going into his arms.

Beau had a drain tube where the third lobe of his right lung had been removed and every time he moved or tried to breathe deeply, he felt a sharp, cutting pain in the area.

Callie was a vision, an angel now. As he'd lost consciousness in that mud and snow covered playground, feeling his breath being stolen out of him, feeling as if he were suffocating, he pictured Callie in his mind, between his tightly shut eyes.

And now she was here, wearing a springtime pink dress just above her knees, those sweet legs of hers smooth and bare. Her red hair was loose and thick around her shoulders, the colors shining copper, gold, and crimson beneath the overhead lights. She was beautiful, and he ached to hold her in his arms once more because he thought he was going to die of his wound.

Tears jammed in his eyes as she drew near and halted at the railing on the left side of his bed, opposite his wound. She leaned over and gently kissed him full on his mouth. His lips were chapped, but hers felt warm, welcoming, and soft against his. Her sweet scent encircled him and he weakly lifted his arms, sliding them around her shoulders as she moaned with joy. Her soft hands framed his face and she kissed him carefully, treating him as if he were fragile. Eyes closing, Beau dealt with the pain of his movement to slide his fingers into her rich, silky long hair, drowning in the heat of her mouth loving his.

Slowly, Callie eased up, opening her eyes that gleamed with unshed tears. "Beau . . . oh, God, you're alive. Thank God! I love you so much."

His voice was rough with emotion as Callie straightened, her hands still entwined in his. "I love you, Callie. I'm gonna be fine, so wipe that frown away, okay?" She tasted of peppermint, and her light, feminine scent was a welcome change to the odor of bleach used to clean the floors nightly.

Callie pulled up a chair and then released the rail, pushing it down carefully so as not to jolt him. She sat down, facing him. "How are you really doing? Are you in pain, Beau?"

He rolled his head just a bit. "Nah, just gripping pain where they cut into me. The drain on my right side makes any movement painful, even breathing. The nurse asked me about the level of pain and I lied. I found out if I give it a number above five, they twirl that button on the IV and it knocks me out for three or four hours at a time, which I hate." He squeezed her damp, cool fingers. "I want my head screwed on straight, Callie, so now I lie and tell them it's a three. That way, the opiate doesn't knock me on my butt and I'm conscious longer. I'd rather be awake and alert, despite the pain."

"I understand." Callie anxiously looked at the dressing across the lower third of his torso. Beau wasn't wearing any shirt, his dark-haired chest beautiful to her. He had all kinds of monitors taped on his chest. "How is your breathing?" she asked.

"They say my oxygen level and lung volume are improving by the hour, so that's good news. They make me breathe hourly into that contraption on my rolling tray over there. It helps me expand my lungs, and that's important. They've gotten me up four times a day to walk since I got here."

He took in another careful breath through the cannula that fitted into his nostrils, feeding him a hundred percent pure oxygen. It was an effort to breathe sometimes, and less oxygen meant less energy. He struggled to do as the nurses asked, because that damn drainage tube made every breath feel like a knife slicing into his side.

"You look so tired," she whispered, enclosing his roughened hand within hers.

"I'll bounce back. It's hard to keep a good man down. Don't you know that?" he teased, his voice hoarse.

"Can I get you some water, Beau? Anything?"

He closed his eyes, giving her a slight smile. "No . . . I'm okay. Everything I've ever wanted is sitting right here next to me . . ." and as she watched, he drifted off to sleep.

Callie swallowed hard, watching Beau sleep. The nurse in charge of the ward had warned her and her grandpa that he was still coming out of the shock and trauma, that the surgery had been long and hard on him. She slowly rose, placing his one arm on the bed, being careful not to touch the large dressing on the side of his ribs. She saw bruises on his face and wondered how he'd gotten them. There were scratches along his one arm. He looked pasty, and his gray eyes had been dark with what she realized now was pain.

Leaning down, she slowly raised the rail so he wouldn't accidentally roll over and fall out of bed. Although, Callie doubted Beau would because that wound dressing looked ominous to her.

"He's sleeping again," the nurse said, coming up beside her. "They sleep a lot right after surgery. It's like a roller coaster of wake and sleep for them the first couple of days afterward."

Callie recognized Nurse Evans, an Army captain and RN. "Is he okay? He just suddenly dropped off."

Nodding, Evans looked at all the equipment surrounding the head of the bed and checked all the monitors. "Yes. As long as his blood pressure is steady," she motioned to one instrument, "and it is, he's doing well. But I think he's in more pain than he's admitting," she said, adjusting the opiate on the IV. "What Sergeant Gardner doesn't realize is that the more pain he's in, the slower he'll heal. Since you're his fiancée, you might talk him into sleeping more now, not less." Satisfied, she patted Callie's shoulder. "He's black ops. Those guys are always on the go. They hate being tied to a bed for any reason."

"Can my grandpa come in now to see him?"

"Sure, it's still visiting hours." The nurse pulled over another chair. "You can both sit here with him if you want. Even though he's sleeping, he'll be aware of your presence."

"How can that be?"

Evans looked at the monitors once more. "Because before you arrived, his blood pressure was higher than normal. Now, it's within normal limits. And it's staying there. You're good for him, Ms. McKinley."

Grateful for the nurse's information, she said, "I'll go get my grandpa. How long can we stay?"

"An hour. Then we close it down because the men here need to be fed."

"Is there any way I can talk to his doctor?"

"He'll be making rounds tomorrow morning beginning at 0600, but visitors aren't allowed in until 1000, when he's finished. He'll see you at that time. I understand the patient's parents are arriving tomorrow?"

"Yes."

"That will do him good, too." She smiled a little. "When family and loved ones can visit, these men get better faster. There's less depression, too. It's a huge morale boost for them."

Callie touched Beau's hand. "He feels chilly."

"I'll get one of my orderlies to bring him in another two blankets. It's normal, so don't worry. Keep holding his hand and I'll let Mr. McKinley know you'd like to have him come in."

"Thank you," Callie said, giving her a grateful look. So much of her anxiety and fear were dissolving as she sat there holding Beau's hand, warming it between her own. Soon, a male orderly brought two more blankets, and together they gently placed them around Beau, leaving the dressing over the wound undisturbed. Her grandfather was right behind him, his face unreadable. He was wearing a black Stetson, a white, long-sleeved shirt, a black leather vest, well-worn Levi's, and his ancient boots. He took off his hat as he approached.

"Well," he murmured, coming and sitting down next to her, "he looks a lot better than I thought he would. He's young. He'll bounce back fast," he added, scanning Beau's sleeping features.

"He looks awful," Callie whispered, giving Graham a quick look.

"He's been through a lot," he told her gently. "Getting shot, nearly dying, changes you. I'm sure he's happy to see you, though. Was he conscious when you came in?"

Nodding, she said, "We had a few minutes together. He was so happy to see me."

"Just as much as you were to see him. I

betcha it was hard to keep your hands off him."

Laughing softly, Callie said, "I did get to kiss him. That's all I wanted to do, Grandpa. I needed to tell him I love him so much."

Graham slid his hand across her shoulders. "And he loves you."

"I was so worried before he went back to Afghanistan. I had a horrible feeling about it . . ." and she chewed on her lower lip for a moment.

Patting her shoulder, he said, "That was woman's intuition. When I had to go over to Iraq, Maisy went crazy with worry. She had a dream the night before I got wounded. It came true. Luckily, it wasn't anything like the wound that Beau got."

"Military people and their families go through so much hell."

"Yeah, they do."

Shaking her head, she asked, "Did you find out anything about Beau's prognosis?"

Graham roused himself. "Yes, I snagged his surgeon by sheer luck. He said if there aren't complications, he'll be out of here in about a week. Beau has been here two days. He said they make him get up and walk around because the exercise is key to his bouncing back. Then, they want to keep him here until the wound is closed. They'll take out that drain the day before he leaves. And he'll be released to go home. There's a VA hospital down in Dunmore, south of Black

Mountain where his folks live. It's about forty minutes away from their home, so they'll send him home and he'll have a doc assigned to him at the VA hospital to follow his progress."

"I want to go with him, Grandpa. I mean . . . if Beau's parents don't mind."

"I don't think they will. They're due in here later this evening. I was on the phone with Mr. Gardner out there while you were in here with Beau."

"And you gave him directions to that hotel we're at near the medical center?"

"Yep, sure did. He called me from a pay phone," Graham said. "They don't own a cell phone."

"Beau said they aren't in the computer age. That's okay. There are days when I wish we didn't have cell phones, but mostly I like them because I can talk to Beau and see his face on Skype. That means so much to me."

"I'm sure it meant a lot to him, too."

She placed her hand on her grandfather's arm. "Thanks for coming with me. You really know how to cut through military tape. And you're great at finding places!"

"Once a sniper, always a sniper," he teased gruffly, squeezing her hand. He watched Beau sleeping, observing how his chest rose and fell. "He's breathing easier since that nurse gave him more of his IV meds. Right now, he needs to sleep a lot. And he will."

"Visiting hours are at ten tomorrow morning."

Graham nodded. "Yes, and I think we should go soon, honey. Cletus and Amber will be arriving pretty soon at our hotel and I'd like us to be there to greet them. I'm sure they're worn out and stressed to the max because of all that's happened to Beau. We'll shepherd them around because the D.C. area is a nightmare to drive in."

CALLIE HAD A hotel room with a door between it and her grandfather's room. It was near evening when someone knocked at her main door. Hurrying to it, she opened it up. A huge man in coveralls and a worn brown felt hat stood there. He had a fuzzy black beard and kind blue eyes. Beside him was a woman about three inches shorter, her light brown hair hanging straight to her shoulders, her gray eyes showing stress and exhaustion. She was wearing a blue calico dress that hung on her lean body and fell to her slender ankles, and a pair of simple brown leather shoes.

"Hi, I'm Callie McKinley," she said to the couple.

"We're Cletus and Amber Gardner," he rumbled. He brought his arm around his wife. "It's right nice to meet you, Callie," and he smiled wearily. "I'm sorry we didn't arrive on time. D.C. traffic is all snarled up."

"Don't worry," Callie murmured, "and please, come in." She stood aside, giving them a warm look of hello.

Luckily, her room was a suite and had a comfy couch and three other chairs in the outer area. Callie shut the door and turned.

"Have you gotten your room yet?

Cletus removed his hat and held it in his long, thick fingers, allowing it to hang at his side. "No, not yet. I wanted to make sure we were at the right place."

"The clerk downstairs said the room was being held in our name," Amber volunteered. She had a large red and white knit purse with a canvas strap hanging over her shoulder.

"Okay, that's great. Please sit down and relax a bit. The bathroom is over there if you need it. I'm going to go next door and get my grandpa. I'll be right back. Just make yourselves at home, please."

Callie saw how stressed they were and hesitated. "We just got back from seeing Beau for the first time." She saw Amber halt, fear in her gray eyes. "And he's fine," she added quickly. "He was awake for about five minutes and then dropped off to sleep. The doctors said he'd sleep a lot at first."

Amber squeezed her hands. "Our boy is fine? Really?"

"Yes, he's doing well, Nurse Evans said. Beau knows you're arriving tonight and that you'll see him tomorrow at ten a.m., when visitor's hours begin." She saw Amber's face crumple and huge tears well up in her eyes. Her husband squeezed his wife's shoulders to comfort her.

"See? I told you Beau was as tough as a mean ole mule." He grinned over at Callie. "That's the best news you could've given us, Ms. McKinley."

"Call me Callie, please. Let me get my grandpa and we'll be right back!"

April 6

CALLIE AND GRAHAM stood back the next morning as they walked in and pointed out Beau to his parents at the hospital. She stood there watching Beau's mother, now wearing a bright red and yellow calico dress, lean down and carefully kiss her son on the left side of his unshaven cheek. Beau looked a lot like his mother down to the gray eyes they shared. She saw Cletus, who had also changed clothes, dressed in what she thought might be his best Sunday church clothes, stand back, tears in his eyes as his wife carefully touched Beau's face. Tears burned in her eyes, too, and she looked up at Graham, who was smiling faintly.

"This is so wonderful," she confided to him, her voice wobbling.

"It is, honey. Nothing like the love of your family around you when you're hurting. Beau looks better this morning; don't you think?"

Nodding, Callie watched as Amber moved away to allow her husband to move beside Beau's bed. She was deeply touched when Cletus ran his thick, work-worn hand over his son's hair, lean down, and place a kiss on his brow. Tears warmed her cheeks but she didn't care if anyone saw them. She had always known from the way Beau spoke about his family, that they were close. Now, she was seeing it firsthand and it made her heart swell with love for all of them. This was going to be her new family once she married Beau.

"You know," Graham said quietly to her, "they're fine people. We had a good talk with them last night." He looked down at Callie. "And you did a lot to make them rest easy that Beau was doing fine. That was the right thing to do. I'm proud of you, Callie."

She gripped his hand, squeezing it hard. Callie didn't know what she'd do without him right now. He was built tall and strong like Cletus Gardner, and both men were the same height and shoulder breadth. One was a Marine sniper, the other a skilled furniture maker. "Amber looked so distraught, but I don't blame her. If it hadn't been for your calls to them after he was wounded, they wouldn't have known anything. That would have been horrible stress on them, not knowing."

"Yes. After someone's been wounded, too little information can send you to hell. But, if you're given a bit more, it can keep you from going there," Graham agreed grimly. "I was glad to be able to do it for them. They're suffering enough."

Her heart had turned over with sympathy when she'd seen Beau's parents fussing over him. When his parents were near, she saw a flush appear on his cheeks. She remembered how much she'd looked forward to coming back to the Eagle Feather Ranch after nearly being killed by the Taliban. There really was no place like home.

"Hey," Graham said, leaning over, catching her gaze. "What's say we go to the nurse's station and see what we can find out about Beau's progress? Let him have some quality time with his mom and dad?"

Eagerly, she nodded, and turned and slipped out of the ward with her grandfather.

Nurse Evans lifted her hand in greeting as they drew close to the busy U-shaped nurse's station. A number of nurses were going on and off shift. "He's looking better this morning," she said to Callie as they drew up to the counter. Glancing at the computer, Evans retrieved his stats. "Blood pressure is normal now." She looked up at Callie. "That's your doing, Ms. McKinley," she grinned.

"I'll gladly take the blame," Callie said. "Can you tell us anything about when Beau will be released from here?"

"Sure," Evans said, sitting down at the computer. She studied the screen and then reported, "The doctor saw him this morning at 0600. The dressing was changed and he was pleased with his healing progress. In his notes, he says that Sergeant Gardner could be released seven days from now provided he continues to make this kind of recovery progress."

Graham asked, "And they're sending him home to his family?"

"Yes, sir. There's a VA hospital forty miles south of his home and they'll be receiving him on an outpatient basis." She pressed her finger to the screen. "They've already assigned him a primary care physician, Dr. Jacob Lincoln, along with a follow-up appointment." Looking up at them, she said, "Sergeant Gardner will have a release conference with me and I'll be giving him a packet of papers and information to carry with him to that VA hospital when he goes to see Dr. Lincoln. There are also instructions on how to keep his incision clean and dry, as well as prescriptions for pain medicine and an antibiotic, and all other necessary information."

"So," Graham asked, frowning, "as soon as he gets home, he has to make another trip down to the VA?"

"No, sir. He'll have his first appointment two weeks after his arrival home. It will already be in the computer system. So long as someone can drive him to Dunmore, things should go as planned."

"I can drive," Callie said firmly, giving her grandfather a glance. She saw him give her a pleased look.

"Good enough. We don't recommend flying for a lung patient because of the altitude and pressure it exerts on their lungs. Is someone going to drive him home?"

"We'll have to talk to Beau's family," Callie said.

"Okay, do that and have either them or you get back to me," Evans said.

"We can do that."

"In another thirty minutes he's due to get up and walk the square again," she said, motioning to the halls that lead to and from the desk area. "We're now getting him up every hour he's awake to take him for a walk around the square, going a little farther each time. It keeps blood clots from forming in his lungs and it forces him to breathe more deeply, which is very important for his recovery."

"Can we help with that with him?" Callie asked. "Because I'll be with him at his home helping to take care of him after he gets out of here."

Evans looked at Graham. "Here at the hospital, you need to have your grandfather with you while walking with Beau. That way, if he suddenly gets dizzy or trips, someone big enough is there to help steady and catch him so he doesn't fall and injure himself further."

"We can do that," Graham promised.

April 6

"HOW ARE YOU doing?" Callie asked Beau. It was nearly time for visitors to leave. Cletus and Amber had just left for the day. She and Graham had returned in the late afternoon, giving him and his parents quality time together earlier. As she searched his murky gray eyes, she could see he was exhausted. It showed in the tightness of the flesh across his cheekbones.

"Whipped," Beau admitted, lying back against the raised bed, seeking her fingers and wrapping them in his.

"It's been a hectic day for you."

"My folks have never gone through anything like this before, Callie."

"None of us have."

"That's true, but it has hit them in a way that they're now more aware of my brothers, Coy and Jackson, being in danger all the time, too. My ma, particularly, has been set back by me getting shot. Now she's worrying a lot more about them."

She met and held his half-closed eyes, realizing Beau was going to drop off suddenly and go to sleep. "Your mother is stressed out, but I think she'll be okay," she murmured, moving her fingers along his hand.

"Yeah . . . I'm tired, Callie . . ."

"Close your eyes. I'll sit here with you until 1700, when visiting hours are over." She saw one corner of his mouth weakly hook upward.

"I love you, Callie. You know that, don't you?"

Compressing her lips, she whispered, "I love you more than life itself, Beau. I'm here for you and I will always be loyal to you. You were loyal to me out there when we were running for our lives. You never quit. You took a bullet for me. I know just how much you love me," she encased his hand between hers, "sweet dreams, my lovely man."

Sighing, Beau whispered, "Sweet dreams of you . . ."

She sat there watching him quickly drop off that invisible cliff of sleep, his breath shallowing out, his hand going limp within hers. She gently laid it beside him and stood, drawing up the covers so he'd be warm. Leaning over, she pressed a kiss to Beau's lined brow, inhaling his male scent, allowing it to feather through her and make her heart beat a little harder.

Straightening, Callie thought of how much Beau had taken after his mother. They had the same color of eyes and an oval face. He had his father's black hair, his love of teasing, and his ability to get a smile out of her. He reminded her so much of Beau, who had taken the best from both his parents. She lay her hand on his light green cotton gown, feeling Beau's inherent strength as a man.

Today she'd seen him rally even more than yesterday. Sadly though, the other nine men in the ward had not received any visitors. The orderlies and other medical personnel became their emotional lifelines, instead. They were as wounded as Beau was, or worse, and she could see the depression and loneliness written in every one of their young faces. So many broken dreams here. So many dreams destroyed by an IED or a bullet.

Her gaze swept Beau's relaxed face. He had people who loved him fiercely right here at his bedside. His parents were devoted and kind. Her grandfather felt Beau would heal up faster than usual because of that confluence of people who had supported him after getting shot. Callie believed Graham.

She moved her fingertips lightly across the surface of Beau's cotton gown, absorbing his strong, calm face. He was not model good looking, but she'd never been drawn to the pretty boys who had perfect faces. Beau had a rugged, interesting looking face, his eyes held kindness and the drawl in his voice always soothed her. Any man who could change a baby's diapers and clean out the diaper pail was stellar in her universe, and she smiled faintly, remembering him doing that at Hope Charity in Kabul.

Wanting a lifetime with Beau, she wasn't sure of anything anymore. A bullet had changed the trajectory of their lives, quite literally. Once, it had been neatly laid out when he'd left her family after the Christmas holiday. Now, four months later, change was all Callie knew. That bothered her a lot because she was someone who did better with a fixed day-in and day-out routine. She wasn't flexible like her big sister, Dara, who was highly adaptable.

Beau was like Dara in that respect and Callie wished she could be more like them, but she couldn't. What lay ahead of them? How long would this injury hamper his life? Would it hinder Beau the rest of his life or not? In what way? Callie just didn't know and wished she did.

She'd tried to find his doctor here at the center but that was like trying to find a needle in a haystack. The nurses couldn't answer most of her questions because it was the doctor's role to give her those answers. Feeling frustrated, she kissed Beau's cheek and then gathered up her purse and jacket. Outside, there had been warm April showers all day.

She smiled goodbye to several of the men in their beds. Her heart ached for them and Callie wished she could do or be something for them, too, but it wasn't in the cards. Pushing through the doors of the ward, she saw her grandfather standing near the nurse's station, talking to a new nurse supervisor on duty now. He'd managed to find out a lot more about Beau's condition and the changes that were coming into his life shortly. He looked up, meeting her eyes. Excusing himself from the nurse, he met her.

"Beau sleeping now?" he asked.

"Yes, he dropped off the cliff again," she said, glad that he was helping her on with the jacket over her lightweight pink sweater.

"He'll do that for about a week or two until he starts getting his feet under him. Hungry? There's a Bob Evans restaurant nearby. Are you ready for some home cooking?" he asked, walking with her to the bank of elevators.

"I am," she said. "We need to call Mom and Dad when we get back to our rooms."

"They appreciate your nightly calls," Graham said, placing his hand in the small of her back as they stepped into the elevator.

"Have you talked to Grandma lately?"

"Yep, a little while ago. She's a good fore-man," and he chuckled. "All the wranglers have returned to the ranch full time, and everyone is getting the ranch up to speed after that hard winter. All's well on that front."

They walked out onto the main floor, many civilians as well as military people were coming and going. Graham walked at her side, the crowds heavy, people hurrying and cutting in and out. As they reached the doors, Callie breathed in the April air that was damp from a recent rain. The sky was patches of gray clouds with blue sky peeking out between them. The trees were budding in their green finery for the coming spring, and the lawn was manicured and neatly cut as they walked down the wet sidewalk toward the parking lot. It felt good to inhale fresh air. She was sure Beau missed it as much. He was a country boy at heart.

"How do you think Cletus and Amber are adjusting to city life here?"

Graham's mouth quirked. "Their flank is pretty well overexposed to tell you the truth. Remember? They live on a big, wooded moun-tain surrounded by state and national forest. They're rural people. Cletus is pretty easygoing, but Amber is high strung by all the hustle and bustle of a city like this." He guided her down a wet asphalt row where hundreds of cars were parked in long lines.

"I really like them, Grandpa."

"That's good, because they're going to be your in-laws, Callie."

She frowned. "Grandpa, you said getting hit by a bullet changed you. I worry about how it will change Beau."

Giving her a sidelong glance, Graham halted at the rental car and clicked the key fob to open the doors. "You worried he'll not want to marry you?"

As always, her grandfather got to the heart of things in a hurry. He opened the passenger side door for her and she climbed in. Smoothing her light blue wool slacks with her hand, she waited until he slid in and shut the door. "Yes, I do worry about that . . . and about his falling out of love with me one day."

Snorting softly, Graham started the car and backed out. "If loving or not loving someone hinged on a bullet, then it wasn't love to begin with." He drove down the long row slowly until they were at a crossroads. Looking both ways, he eased out into the rush hour traffic around the medical center, which was bumper to bumper.

"I feel like he still loves me, but I'm scared, Grandpa. Scared that somehow, this changes how he sees me. Sees us . . ."

Drawing in a breath, Graham said, "His healing is going to take time, Callie. He almost died, and believe me, almost dying will change us. He's going to have nightmares about this and PTSD symptoms, for sure. He's going to go up and down like a barometer emotionally for months to come."

"You went through this."

"Yes, I did. And your grandmother was at her wits end sometimes with me because I was swinging emotionally back and forth like a yoyo," he said. "I never doubted for a moment that I didn't love her, but she had a man she thought she knew come home to her very changed, and unlike the person she used to know. She thought for the longest time I no longer loved her. It was a very hard time for both of us."

Clasping her hands in her lap, Callie stared at the traffic all around them. "Did you ever want to split up? Quit?"

He held her gaze. "Yes, several times. I won't lie to you, Callie, this is going to be a rough road for you both. But you have McKinley genes and you're strong as titanium. What you have to do is be there for him when he needs you. Listen to him. Ask a lot of questions. Don't assume anything because if you do, you'll probably be wrong and that's going to create all kinds of stress and anxiety between the two of you.

He's going to connect you with other events and people in his past he can depend on when he's tired, stressed, hurting, and feeling death stalking him again. He'll know that you are there, steady, and strong for him. It's not an easy hurdle to leap. Nor is it easy to appear to be strong all the time, because you won't be. No one can do that. So, it's a lot of ups and downs. The best thing you can do is talk a lot. If you don't? It could split any couple apart."

"Was Grandma the one who wanted to give up?"

"No, it was me, Callie. I was so deep into my own pig wallow, so blinded by all that I'd seen and lived through, that I was lost for a good year or more. I was black ops just like Beau. And he's seen just as much as I have. This wound he nearly died from is going to rake him over Hell itself. And you're going to have to be there for him. But it's hard, honey. So damned hard."

CHAPTER 5

April 17

BEAU LISTENED TO the plop, plop, plop of raindrops falling from the mid-April sky on the cabin sitting on Black Mountain. The cedar shakes on the roof were absorbing most of the sound. He lay partially sitting up, each breath painful. Closing his eyes, feeling the utter exhaustion of the last two weeks, he was glad to finally be home. It had taken his parents driving him home to get here, four days after being released from the military hospital. This small guest cabin had one bedroom and was about a thousand square feet, all told. His father had built it when he was in his late teens.

The old brass bed where he was laying was surrounded with goose-down pillows to support him. He reached out with his left hand, moving it across the old, thin bedspread. His grandmother,

Bess Gardner, had made it fifty years ago, and it showed its age. He'd grown up with in on his bed at his parents' cabin, and on nights when he had nightmares, which wasn't very often, he'd bundled himself up in it, pulling into a fetal position, clutching the warm, colorful quilt around him like a shield. Then feeling secure, he'd promptly fallen asleep.

He fondly remembered his grandmother. She'd lived to be a hundred and two, with lively blue eyes like his father's, her black hair streaked with silver. And she'd loved her three grandsons, always giving them big, smacking kisses on the cheek and forehead whenever they came close to her. His mother now had every one of Bess's quilts. They were heirlooms, precious mementos of an earlier time that Amber wanted passed down through the generations, along with the colorful stories about Gram Bess.

Now, Beau moved his fingers across the thinning cotton, still strong after so many decades. He could remember as a boy when electricity still hadn't been strung across Black Mountain. Then, they'd used a washboard, washing one section of the big quilt at a time on it.

The rain soothed his rattled mind, his fingers splayed out against the quilt. The cabin was cool, with only a wood stove for heating. Although the April weather was above freezing, the cabin was usually chilly if the wood stove hadn't been fired up.

In the other room, Callie slept on a couch his father had made for Gram Bess decades earlier. It was a good, long couch, hardly showing any age. The black walnut wood shining from being oiled by hand. Amber had made the comfortable cushions placed across the sofa and had sewn them on a special Singer machine that handled heavy fabric. All was quiet, and he hoped Callie was sleeping well.

Even sighing caused a stabbing pain in his lung. The VA doc told him it was from where the drain had been inserted. In time, the pain would disappear as the wound healed. He looked down at the thick, white dressing across the right side of his ribcage. Callie changed it daily, but it was Poppy Thorn, a Black Mountain hill doctor, who had met them when they'd arrived home, who would provide medical assistance. Her daughter, Baylee Ann Thorn-Griffin, a former 18 Delta Navy corpsman, was also helpful.

The women taught Amber and Callie how to change his dressing daily and how to look for redness, heat, or swelling, which could indicate infection. They also took his temperature several times a day. If infection occurred, they would have to rush him down to the VA hospital in Dunmore to get him emergency treatment. And this happened, Amber was to call Baylee immediately. She and her husband, Gabe, an ex-SEAL, would drive down to the cabin and drive Beau to the hospital. Just knowing this gave them all more confidence that they could handle whatever came up.

Beau pulled his left arm across his eyes, feeling lost. He wasn't alone, and for that, he was grateful. But the last two weeks had twisted him into a knot. Everyone, since he had come home, walked on eggs around him. Beau could see the anxiety in them, the fear that something might go wrong, throwing him into another life-and-death battle. He ached to have Callie lying next to him, her head resting on his shoulder, her arm across his torso, naked and warm against the hard length of his body. His mouth tightened and he felt hot tears well up, but fought them back.

Beau knew his father was a big believer in men crying. He had taught his sons it was okay to let go. He'd seen his father cry. Tears leaked beneath his short, spiky lashes, trailing down his recently shaved face. Earlier tonight, Callie had shaved him, and he had looked forward to it so much—her tender touch, her smile.

But there was no manual on how to act or feel after you'd survived a near-lethal attack. These days, Beau's moods were up and down. One hour, he was higher than a damned kite, feeling lucky to be alive and surrounded by so many people that he loved. The next hour, he felt as if he'd stepped off a cliff into a deep black hole. It was those "down times" that Nurse Evans had warned him about. How he hated these moments of deep depression. Beau had never dealt with anything like this before. He had always been a mellow, happy guy, known for his optimistic outlook. Until now.

Anger and frustration thrummed through him. Callie had repeatedly tried to talk to him about how he was doing, but he clammed up. No one knew what combat was like, but she did, having gone through that ambush and escape from the Taliban last November.

A few minutes later, exhausted by his memories of the past and his frustrations in the present, Beau dropped off to sleep.

CALLIE NEARLY JUMPED off the couch when she heard Beau cry out. She hurried into his room and saw that the clock on his dresser read four a.m. There was a small night light plugged into the wall, and Beau was barely visible. But she could see that his skin was glistening with sweat and he'd torn off his covers. He wore a set of pajama trousers and his feet stuck out between the rumpled covers. Beau was breathing hard, a moan of pain tearing from between his tightened lips. And he was awake.

"Beau? It's Callie. You're okay," she whispered, moving to his right side, her gaze dropping to the dressing. Bay Griffin had told her to watch for any new, fresh blood stains on that white gauze dressing. If there were any, she was to call her on her cell phone and she'd quickly come down to see what had been torn apart. To her relief, the dressing was white, not red. Reaching out, she saw the agony in his shadowed eyes. She slid her fingertips across his sweaty brow, placing the damp strands back into place. "Nightmare?" she guessed.

"Yes," he gritted out, shutting his eyes, tensing because the pain was sharp and jabbing in the area of his lung.

"What can I do?" She'd learned from Bay what kind of questions to ask Beau. Otherwise, she'd feel panic instead. She continued to slide her hand over his hair in light, gentle caresses. Her touch always soothed him. She waited. Right now, his eyes were tightly shut as he wrestled with the pain of breathing deeply. His flesh was pasty and she knew that was a sign of deep pain. She'd learned not to blurt out a fix for it, but it was hard not to ask if he wanted medication to dull it.

"Just . . . nothing," he rasped, his breath still ragged, his chest heaving.

"Okay," she soothed. Leaving his side, she pulled up the blankets, settling them over him to his waist, wanting to keep him warm. The cabin was deeply chilled and felt damp. She needed to make a fire in the wood stove to drive it away. Bay had worried about Beau catching pneumonia if he wasn't in a warm, dry environment and these cabins were poorly insulated.

She smoothed her hand down his right arm, feeling the sweat. He gripped her fingers in his, feeling his anxiety. What had he been dreaming about? The firefight where he got wounded? Most likely, but Callie said nothing except to place her other hand on his naked shoulder to stabilize him.

Beau didn't want anything atop his skin but a lightweight sheet across his wound area. The weight of blankets bothered him and he couldn't stand it, pulling them away from his chest. Callie badly wanted to lean over and hold Beau because she knew that's what he needed, but with that chest wound, she couldn't. Instead, she continued to move her hand lightly across his shoulder, some of the sweat dissipating, his breathing beginning to slow down. Beau lay against the wall of pillows that kept him upright. She knew better than to try to rearrange them when he was enmeshed in an emotional storm. Bay had urged her to simply be there, remain quiet, and keep her touch and connection with him. That was what Gabe, her husband, had done for her when she'd had flashbacks of her rape and capture by the

Taliban. Just his closeness to her, someone she considered safe, helped her reorient and come out of those horrifying memories.

Callie wished she could say or do something, but she knew by now that words didn't always carry the weight that her touch did. She had never realized just how important it was until now. Beau responded quickly to her hand on his shoulder and he collapsed against the pillows, eyes shut, his breathing slowing down.

How like animals we all are, Callie thought. She was raised on a ranch, and had helped birth the calves, foals, puppies, and kittens. All of them reacted positively to touch, people were no different, she realized. She felt Beau's fingers grow stronger around hers, giving them a squeeze. She smiled a little into his shadowy, tense face. "What can I do for you, Beau?" she asked again.

He frowned, barely opening his eyes. Rolling his head toward her, he rasped, "I'd give *anything* for you to lie beside me. I need you, Callie."

Her heart tore open as she remembered their time together, body-to-body, skin-on-skin, holding him in her bed. "I know, it seems like a dream from the past, doesn't it?"

Grimacing, Beau rasped, "Yeah, a beautiful dream . . ."

"Is there anything you'd like that I can bring you, besides me?" she shot him a grin to help lighten the mood. "A drink of water?" Callie knew from past nightmares that he was now grounded and back here with her.

"Yeah. Water, please?"

She retrieved a glass of water with a straw, brought it over to him, and pressed the straw between his lips. He drank in gulps, emptying the glass.

"More?" she asked gently.

He nodded, wiping his mouth with his left hand. Following her with his eyes, he watched her pour another glass of water from a nearby plastic pitcher. "I don't know what I'd do without your help, Callie. Thank you."

"I want to be right here beside you, Beau. I love you, and I want to help you as much as I can." Turning, she held the glass for him and allowed him to drink until he was sated. Color was slowly starting to return to his cheeks, and she felt tiny tendrils of relief.

"Thanks," he whispered. He watched her set the glass down on the bed stand. "I'm sorry I woke you."

"*I'm* not, big guy. I love spending time with you. Do you want anything else?"

"Yeah, you." He managed a weak, teasing smile, turning his right hand over resting it on the mattress. "Just you."

"You have me," she said. "Always. Meanwhile, are you warm enough, Beau? Do you want me to start a fire in the wood stove?"

"No, thanks. I'm fine. Give me your hand," he replied, stretching out his open palm.

Sliding her fingers into his, she stood above him and saw the exhaustion shadowing Beau's face. "How's the pain level in that lung?"

"Bearable."

Shaking her head, she said, "Beau, you don't have to tough this out. You know the doctor said you could take that pain med. You'll heal up faster if you aren't in pain all the time."

She saw his eyes flicker with frustration and knew it had to do with his ego. Baylee had told her that men would always want to tough it out. She'd seen it as a combat medic again and again. Callie appreciated her wisdom and experience. It helped her understand why Beau was being so stubborn about admitting he was in pain. It was the "manly" thing to do, and it made her want to scream in frustration.

She had a sudden inspiration. "How about," she posed, "if I give you *half* a pain pill? That way, it won't knock you out for hours." She saw him consider it. Sometimes, Callie felt like a horse trader with Beau. Knowing he wasn't doing it on purpose, that he was still in recovery, and dealing with trauma, she could easily forgive him.

"Well . . . yeah . . . that would be okay, I guess . . ."

She smiled a little. "I'll be right back."

Returning from the bathroom, she put half the pill on his tongue and gave him water to wash it down.

"You'll feel better now," she soothed, setting the glass aside.

"I want you so damned badly beside me, Callie."

"I know you do. But until that lung heals up more, I can't do it. Every time I move beside you I'd be aggravating your wound. You'd never get any sleep, Beau." She saw his brows draw down, frustration gleaming in his eyes.

"You didn't sign on for this," he muttered.

"No, but you didn't either," she reminded him. "You didn't join the Army to get shot."

"I knew as a Delta operator the potential was there, though."

Her lips puckered. "Well, I knew when I fell in love with you that as a black ops man, you'd always be in harm's way, and that you could get wounded, or worse, killed." She leaned over and brushed his lips. Once she'd kissed him, she drew back, her lips a mere quarter of an inch from his, and added, "And I weighed all of that before I let all my love carry me away to you, Beau Gardner."

She felt him relax even more. Maybe it was her kiss, her loving him from a distance, or maybe it was the meds. She wasn't sure. He lifted his left hand slowly, because any movement of his rib cage inspired pain in his wound, his fingers sliding through her thick, crimson strands. She smiled, eyes closed. They both needed this intimacy with one another. It fed them, and kept their hope strong and bright with one another.

"I wish I could love you right now, Beau," she whispered against his lips. She felt him smile a little beneath her mouth.

"Do you want the truth? I haven't had one sexual thought since I got hit."

Easing away, she laughed. "Well, I'm not surprised. Almost dying kind of takes precedence, doesn't it?"

"I guess," he grumped. "I'm just not the man I used to be, Callie."

"What do you mean?"

"Well, I can't love you. I can't hold you. You pull down my trousers and briefs so I can pee or poop. There's just a boxcar load of things I can't do anymore by myself."

"But in time, you'll be able to pull down your jeans and briefs to go to the bathroom, Beau. You will be able to hold me and love me, and I'll love you back."

She saw the devastation and loss in his eyes. The meds were indeed starting to take over because he was far more willing to talk with her. She cherished these moments with him. They were too far and few between.

"I guess . . . I guess I didn't see this coming, Callie." He looked up into her eyes, worry in them.

Shrugging, she sighed. "My parents and grandparents taught me there was nothing fixed about a person's life path, Beau. Things happen, both good and bad, to all of us, all the time. If you hadn't been in the Army, if you hadn't been protecting Hope Charity from that Taliban attack, you could have been a civilian instead and gotten into a car wreck."

"Well, shit happens," he muttered darkly, "for sure." Beau didn't usually curse around her, and she knew he was sinking into a heavy place.

"Hey," she said, "we'll work through this together. Like we've done everything else." There was a question in his eyes and she wasn't sure what that was about. He said the words, *I love you*, to her, but sometimes, she wondered if he was just saying it and not meaning it. That scared her as nothing else. She wanted to ask him more questions, but Callie knew he was exhausted from lost sleep and desperately needed to get some.

"We'll tackle it all together," she promised him softly, leaning over, kissing his brow. "I'm in this with you forever, Beau. I'm not leaving your side. I'm here for the long haul." Callie's family had taught her commitment, hanging in through the rough times, and being grateful for the good times. She'd grown up seeing that time and again with the family that surrounded her and Dara.

"That's good to hear, sweetheart."

Caressing his cheek, she whispered, "Go to sleep, Beau. I'll stand here for a bit. Close your eyes, okay?"

And he did. Within a minute, Callie watched him drop off that invisible cliff, his body sag, all the tension draining from him. She slowly loosened her fingers from his and brought up the sheet to cover his chest.

Tiptoeing quietly out of his room, she went back to her couch bed and lay down. It was almost five a.m., but the skies around Black Mountain were still dark. As Callie snuggled down beneath the quilt and sheet, nestling into the goose down pillow, she pretended she was lying next to Beau.

May 15

BEAU WALKED SLOWLY, Callie's hand around his leather belt to catch him in case he fell. The May afternoon sunlight fell in shadows around the Gardner homestead that comprised ten acres of Black Mountain. They lived on the lower slope of the mountain, the area thick with elm, oak, poplar, and maple. The ground was uneven, sticks and sometimes rocks hidden by leaves here and there. Beau had to walk every hour he was up because it improved his lung function. Today, he wore a bright red t-shirt, his jeans, and hiking boots. On his head, as always, was his frayed Army green baseball cap. She smiled to herself, glad to have his left arm around her shoulders, walking so closely together.

"Someone had to do a lot of leveling out of this slope," she said, gesturing with her left hand toward the huge five-acre garden, "to make it flat so water would stay in there and soak in."

"That was my great-grandparents, Sally and Eli," he told her. "They bought the land and Eli had a team of mules and a plow. It took him two years to take the slope off our homestead," Beau told her, "and make it flat like we see it nowadays."

"That had to be a lot of work."

"It was. He also built the main cabin where my folks live and where we boys were born and grew up."

"What about that little cabin we're in?" She lifted her face, feeling the warmth of the sunlight falling upon it. The rain had cleared up in the early morning, the mid-morning temperature now in the high sixties.

"My pa engaged the three of us boys and we built it. He wanted to teach us how to build a log cabin and we learned."

"What was the purpose of that cabin?" Callie wondered as she felt Beau slow to a halt. Every day he challenged himself to walk a little farther, making his lungs work, and open up to their full capacity to take oxygen into his body.

"My parents were hoping one of us boys would marry and want to come back here to live. He told us it was a 'starter' cabin, something we could build onto when we brought our brides home. There's plenty of land to add on bedrooms or whatever else was needed later on."

She looked up at him, seeing that same strength in his face, feeling her need of him, and enjoying time and space with Beau. Keeping her arm around his waist, she asked, "Did you want to be the one to come home?"

He turned, studying her. "I never knew what would happen to me in that regard, Callie. When I saw you, everything fell into place for me. You were the woman I wanted for my wife. Wanted forever." He squeezed her gently against him, kissing the top of her head.

Warming to his intimate words, she reflected that only in the past few days had Beau once more reached out for her. He had told her that after a major wounding the intimacy they once shared would slowly return, that she would be giving him much more than he could give her at first. Now, just having him tall and strong against her felt so good, so right. She hungered for moments like this and was relieved that they were appearing more often.

"I'm glad you saw me belly dance," she teased, smiling up at him. He'd taken her advice from that night weeks ago, using half of a pain med near noon. Callie had breathed a sigh of relief. It had been a good call because he was sleeping at night, and sleep was healing. When Beau was in pain, he was distracted and not available to her. He was being more amenable about taking half a med rather than none. Maybe it was the healing curve that Bay had talked about.

"Me too," he replied softly, watching a robin sailing across the meadow surrounded by thick woods on all sides.

She felt a sadness within Beau despite the warm sunlight that felt so good. She could feel him absorbing the sun, drinking it in, and loved the fact that he was an outdoors lover as much as she was. Fresh air and sunlight were healing to everyone.

"It's a beautiful day, isn't it, Beau? So why are you feeling so sad?"

He held her a little more tightly. "I don't know. It just comes in waves, Callie. I wish I could control it, but I can't."

"It happened to me," she admitted, meeting his darkening gray eyes. "After I nearly got raped in that ambush."

"It did?" She could tell she had his attention now.

"I felt like I was flying apart inside, Beau. I couldn't control my emotions, my fear of dying, or my fears that I'd never see you or my family again. I couldn't cry enough. It would come and go at the oddest times. One moment I was up and giddy with happiness that I was alive, in the next I'd crash and burn."

"When I came to visit you for Christmas, these were the feelings you were struggling with?

"Yes." She gave him a painful look. "I was a hot mess."

"Funny, that's how I've felt since regaining consciousness in Germany at the medical center."

"I still have it, Beau. It's not as bad or as intense or as often, but I have hours when I wrestle with it."

"This must be PTSD?"

"I don't know. I was talking with Bay the other day about it after she finished checking your dressings. We went outside to the corral where the sheep are kept and just stood talking. I told her about my emotions. I thought they were PTSD and she said no, that they're just plain old human emotional reaction to trauma and thinking I was going to die."

"Huh," Beau said, frowning. "Did Bay say how long it would last, because it sucks."

Giving him a faint smile, Callie said, "Bay said it's different for everyone."

"I never knew you were struggling with things like that. Why didn't you tell me this was how you were feeling, Callie?" he asked, searching her eyes.

Shrugging, she whispered, "I just felt so messed up, Beau, that I thought you'd see me as a whiner. That I wasn't strong enough to gut through this."

He stared at her and then grew frustrated. "And I never asked you how you felt, either. That's on me. Dammit."

He was upset. Callie smoothed her palm against his back. "Hey, don't go there, okay? We led such stressful lives at that time, Beau. My grandpa tried to pull it out of me, but I wouldn't talk, even to him."

"You asked me just now about myself and my feelings, Callie."

"Because I've been through what you're going through, that's why. I wanted to talk to you, Beau, but I was afraid you'd think less of me."

He laughed, relief tinging his words. "Well, I guess I'm in the same boat that you are. I was afraid to say anything for the very same reasons. I felt you'd think less of me," he admitted with an apologetic look.

"Geez Gardner, you know I think you're a hero ten times over from the time I met you!" Callie released him, hand on his left elbow as she walked in front of him and then halted. "Beau, you saved my life. I'd already fallen for you before that ambush. I thought by my stupid decision to run I had exposed both of us to a life-

and-death situation, and that you'd want me out of your life forever. You took a bullet in your calf for me."

Her voice grew hoarse as she clung to his gaze. "I put your life in jeopardy. I still live with that to this day. There are times," she choked, "that I don't know why you continue to love me, Beau. I almost got you killed."

"Now, Callie," he soothed, gripping her hand, kissing the back of it, "don't you dare go there. You're a civilian, you're not a military person. You've never been trained up to deal with what got thrown at you in that ambush. I'll never hold that against you, ever. You did your best and it was damn good! Do you hear me?"

She swallowed, avoiding his intense gaze, the urgency in his voice. Callie lifted her chin, holding his stare. "I hear you, Beau."

"Never question my love for you, all right? Never." He relaxed his hand around hers, releasing it. Even lifting his left arm caused a lot of discomfort to his rib cage. "After I got hit in the side, I was having a lot of trouble breathing. I lay there stunned, unable to move. Every breath I took, Callie, I thought was my last."

He heard her gasp, throwing her hand up across her mouth, her green eyes going wide. Pushing on, he said roughly, "I knew I was dying. I could feel it. Every breath was less and less. I had blood coming up out of my right lung, filling my mouth and I was choking on it. My last thoughts, sweetheart, were of you." He reached out, touching her hair and cupping her cheek, holding her tear filled eyes. "I now understand what you went through, Callie. You thought you were going to die, too. None of this diminished one whit about how I feel toward you. If anything my love is stronger for you now than it ever was." He leaned over, very carefully, and kissed her mouth, moving against her lips, feeling her returning warmth. God! Didn't she know he needed her more than life itself?

CHAPTER 6

May 20

"COME ON. LET'S sit down on the swing," Callie urged Beau.

Up ahead of him, in an area between the chicken coop and corrals with the barn, sat an ancient elm with thick, spreading limbs. Rallying, Beau nodded, taking her hand and walking toward it. Right now, he was a mess inside, beating himself up for not having been sensitive to Callie's struggles. But he had been. He'd done so much to support her during that period.

Since she had admitted it nearly a week ago, he'd chewed on it. She'd been an emotional wreck after the ambush in Afghanistan and he'd been unsure how to help her get through it. He'd not known what to do, what to ask her, or what to say. Callie never blamed him for it. In part, it was her fault because she never shared how she was feeling with him.

They slowly walked across the gravel park-
way between the swing and the main cabin. Beau
had begun to recognize how important it was for
those who experienced trauma to have a sound-
ing board, just as Callie was for him. She'd
suffered in silence. Callie was teaching him to be
transparent, that it was all right to unveil his
deepest feelings to her.

His fingers tightened around hers. The pain
in his heart was more acute than the jabbing pain
he experienced each time he placed his right boot
on the ground, activating pain in his injured lung.
The crunch of the gravel was drowned out by a
red rooster crowing in the hen house area. A
couple of sheep, which his mother kept for
shearing twice a year for blankets, called back, as
if to answer the rooster.

Sitting down in the ancient swing made by
his grandfather always gave Beau a sense of
peace. Thick chains held the large swing beneath
an overhead limb, and Beau sat on one end, his
right elbow on the wooden arm because it
stabilized his healing rib cage. Callie, who wore a
pair of pecan colored twill pants, sat facing him,
one leg beneath her. The spring breeze lifted
strands of her hair, now glowing crimson and
gold as sunlight shot through them. Beau swore
she looked like an angel with a halo of light
around her head.

"Comfy?" she asked him, resting her hands in her lap about a foot away from where he sat.

"Yeah, I've always liked this swing." He casually glanced in her direction and was relieved to see the tension dissolving from her features. Placing his hand over her knee closest to him, he added, "As a kid, I liked coming out here after our chores were done for the day. I'd watch the clouds come overhead and find images of animals and insects in them. Sometimes, I'd even see a face."

"Funny," she said, leaning against the back of the swing, "I used to do the same thing up at our ranch. I had a small hill where I rode one of our horses. I loved doing it all summer long. And like you, once I got my chores done, I'd tell my mom where I was going and take off across the pastures to my hiding place."

"It wasn't much of a hiding place, though," Beau teased, grinning.

Laughing, Callie agreed, "No, everyone knew where it was. Dara and I were trained from early on to always let our parents and grandparents know exactly where we were going."

"You had a nice time growing up, so did I," and he gave his home a wistful look. "There are so many memories here. Good ones."

"Amber said that your grandparents used to live in that other cabin where your father now makes his furniture?"

"Yes." Beau looked at the third cabin that sat off to one side of the property. "Eli and Sally Gardner built that cabin together. After he homesteaded this land, one of the requirements was to put a building on it to prove you were using the land and not squatting on it."

"Why do you think they made it so long? It's like one long room."

"I don't know. It served them, though. My pa loves the way it's built because he can completely assemble and make couches, chairs, and cabinets in there. There's plenty of space for all his tools and equipment, and for his projects in the works for other folks."

"He's magical with his hands and wood," Callie agreed, impressed by what she had seen since she'd arrived. "I love going in there to see what he's working on."

"My pa is an artist. But my Great-Grandpa Eli was too." He lifted his left hand. "I didn't get that gene."

"You do other things very well," Callie said.

He became somber. "I look at what I do— and I take lives, Callie. I'm not saying those evil bastards didn't deserve to leave this earth, because they did. If they're left alive, they'll make so many other people suffer. I'm not sorry I took them out."

She studied him as a light breeze sifted overhead, moving the newly sprouting leaves. "Are you looking at what you're doing with your life? I know I did."

"Yes," he said, frowning. "Coming here is peaceful. There's no strife, no threat to home and family."

"That's the way I felt when I returned from Afghanistan after that ambush. I was never so glad to get back to our ranch as I was then, Beau. It meant peace and quiet, and I knew I could let down and finally let go."

"I was so glad to see you leave Afghanistan," he murmured, meeting her sad gaze. "You turned the corner when you got home, though." He lifted his head, gazing across the huge gravel circle, the corral, barn, and cabins on the other side. "I guess I never realized how much home meant to me until just now."

"It's a haven to heal up in," Callie offered. "Your parents are so happy that you're with them."

"There was so much stress on 'em after I got shot," he said, frowning.

"This experience will change you, Beau. And them. I know it's changed me."

"I can feel the changes inside me, Callie. They're not that clear yet. I don't see them, but I feel my life turning around. When I was lying in that playground, gasping like a fish thrown onto the ground, I remember thinking I didn't want to die. I had you. I loved my brothers, my folks. I just wanted to go home. All I could think of was your smile, walking our acreage here at home, helping my pa sand down some wood he was working on, or helping my ma can vegetables or fruit in the kitchen. I remembered thinking it was all over."

"Were you scared?"

"No. Long ago, Callie, I knew I could die because of the career I'd chosen. I was at peace with that. What startled me was that I wasn't ready to die. I wanted to be at home with you in my arms, and I had to see you carrying our children. I wanted to watch them grow up and be happy, like I was while growing up." He shook his head and pushed the rocker with the toe of his boot a little bit.

"I wanted to make you happy. I remember as I lost consciousness I saw your smile, how bright, sunny, and beautiful it was. I heard you calling to me." Beau gave her a sideward glance to gauge her reaction. He saw Callie's lips part in shock.

"Yeah, I felt you with me, Callie. Honest to God, I did. I could feel you kneeling beside me, your knees against my back to keep me on my injured right side, your one hand on my upper arm, the other cradling beneath my head. You kept telling me to breathe, to hold on, that help was coming, that I wasn't going to die because you loved me."

Callie stared. "I-I never knew that . . ."

He squeezed her fingers. "I wanted to tell you when I felt the time was right. We're beyond the crisis now and I'm at a stage where I'm starting to heal up. You were there with me. I felt the indent of your knees into my back to hold me steady and stay on my right side. I felt the strength of your hand around my arm, Callie. You were holding me in a position that allowed me to breathe instead of drown in my own blood. I asked Nurse Evans about that back at Bethesda. She said pushing me onto my wounded side allowed me to get enough air out of the good left lung." He gave her a long, warm look. "You saved my life this time around, sweetheart, whether you knew it or not."

Shaken, Callie stared at him open mouthed. "T-T-that's . . . unbelievable . . . wonderful . . . did you tell Nurse Evans about it?"

"I did."

"What did she say?"

"Well, I thought she was gonna laugh at me, but she became very serious. She said she'd heard other men who were badly wounded have a loved one come to their side, comfort them, talk to them, and tell them to hold on, too. I wouldn't have believed it if it hadn't happened to me." Beau held her luminous gaze. "Callie, I could feel you infusing me with life. I could feel how hot your hands were around my arm and my head. I could feel powerful waves of energy coursing through me from your hands. I can't explain it. But it happened. It wasn't a dream. Maybe my head was all screwed up and I imagined it, but to this day, I believe you saved my life. Now, we're even," he said, giving her a crooked grin.

Beau saw the surprise in Callie's face, her lovely green eyes huge with disbelief. Her expression was one of wonder and awe. That was how he had felt when it happened. "She urged me to share it with you. Nurse Evans said that if I told my doc, he'd explain it away as nerve firings in my brain causing the hallucination, but she told me to hold on to it and remember it just as it happened. It was so real, Callie. I swear to God, it was."

She sat there for a long time, staring off into the springtime afternoon, absorbing Beau's revelation.

"I remember nothing about it," she said. "But you know what? My grandpa always said that love could push back death."

Beau nodded. He knew Graham was a black ops Marine sniper who had seen the worst of the Gulf War in Iraq. He'd almost died on a later mission. "Has Graham ever talked to you about the time he was shot?"

"No. Ever since I came home from surviving that ambush, he's opened up a lot more to me about what he did over there. But just snippets, not much detail."

"Has he ever talked to you about his wife after he got shot and was bleeding out?"

Callie gave him a searching look. "No. Why?"

"Sometime, when it feels right, tell your grandpa about my experience with you coming to my side and holding me in the right position so I could breathe and live until help could arrive. Okay?"

Callie gave him a curious look. "I will."

"Every day, I'm more and more convinced it wasn't my imagination," Beau murmured, looking away, watching the sheep in the corral. "It was real. I know it was. I felt you there. You leaned over me, your hair was loose, and it tickled the side of my face, Callie. I felt your warm breath against my temple when you were telling me to relax, to just breathe and not move, that help was on the way. That was as real as me holding your hand right here and now."

June 1

BEAU WATCHED AS Callie got down on her hands and knees in the huge five-acre garden along with his mother. He sat near his father's furniture-making cabin, hearing his radio playing bluegrass music. His ma's male yellow tabby cat, Butch, sauntered in, his crooked tail waving languidly from side to side. Butch had wandered

into their lives five years earlier. He was a stray
tom, his face beaten up, scratches all over it, one
ear missing, but he was a formidable gopher
hunter, and he kept Amber's garden rid of
gophers.

The sunlight felt wonderful as he leaned
against the side of the cabin, his face tipped up,
absorbing the rays. Callie's laughter mingled with
his ma's, and he smiled. It was getting easier to
take in a full breath of air, finally, and there was
no longer pain as he inhaled. He was glad that the
VA had finally released him because he'd hated
the place. His appointments were always being
cancelled and rescheduled, only to be cancelled
again. Thanks to Bay Griffin's expertise as a
combat medic, Beau was on a solid healing curve.
She came down twice a week to examine the scar
alongside his ribs, check his heart, blood pressure, and press here and press there. The VA was
letting vets fall through the cracks, and some had
died. He hadn't, thank God, because Bay tended
him—one vet helping another.

Callie worked in concert with Bay. Beau continued to use his breathing apparatus, having to
blow into it and force the total inflation of his
lungs. She made sure he did the exercises like
clockwork, every day. The woman he loved was
now a seamless part of his family. Amber had
taught Callie how to crochet and often, if they
weren't out weeding the garden, he could find

them in that swing beneath the limbs of the elm, crocheting and talking.

Slowly, he was emerging from his personal hell. Gabe Griffin, Bay's husband, came down at least once a week just to visit with him. They would sit outdoors, sometimes walking the nearby trails, and talk. Gabe had gone through his own dark place, and it was easier to share his feelings with the ex-SEAL. Feeling guilty that he couldn't do the same thing with Callie, Beau was afraid that his description of how he'd nearly died had already upset her. It didn't upset Gabe, who had seen it all, because he was a black ops brother.

His earlier magnetism to Callie had shifted since he'd nearly died. Now, he salivated like a starving wolf to be around her. Cherishing her laughter, the sparkle in her green eyes, that wicked smile of hers, lifted him as never before. In some ways, he felt like a male Persephone from Greek mythology.

Persephone was the daughter of Mother Earth, Ceres. Hades, the god of Hell, had lusted after young, beautiful Persephone and kidnapped her, taking her to his underground lair where he lived inside the dark, sunless earth.

At first, because she'd been kidnapped, she pined away for her mother, for sunlight, and fresh air. She became depressed. No matter what Hades tried to do to lift her spirits, nothing worked. She was slowly dying before his eyes and he felt helpless. Finally, he went to her mother, Ceres, and asked her what to do. The mother made a deal with Hades: let her daughter live above the earth with her for two seasons out of the year. The other two seasons, she would live inside the earth, in the darkness, with him. Hades took the deal to Persephone, who instantly agreed to it. She came alive again, filled with hope and infused with life once more. When she came above the earth, spring and summer flourished. When she went below to live with Hades, fall and winter came to the planet.

Beau felt a lot like the young goddess. His life had been hijacked by that bullet, changed forever. He'd never known depression before and it was Bay who diagnosed it. It was some-thing he'd live with while he wrestled silently within his own psyche about nearly dying. Bay knew about almost dying, too. And she shared her deep, dark bouts with him. After hearing her trials, Beau didn't feel so alone. And he began to understand the process that he was slogging his way through, one agonizing step at a time. Bay and Gabe had gone through their own ups and downs. Bay pointed this out one day to Beau had Callie, and that they still loved one another. She'd found that having Gabe, and their love for one another, helped her get through those dark patches, which still came and went. She could not control them, she told him, and neither would he. But when he found himself falling into that dark abyss of depression, he should reach out for Callie and draw her tightly to him. "Talk to her, let it all hang out. And don't worry what she might think of the dark places you have to travel through sometimes," added Bay firmly.

Drawing in a long, slow breath, Beau opened his eyes, knowing he had to share his concerns with Callie. He'd been hiding so much from her and he knew it hurt her. He could see the anguish in her eyes sometimes, wanting to ask him questions, but holding back and asking nothing.

She'd learned early on that if she pushed him with too many questions, he would snarl and became irritable, even angry with her. Then, looking sad, she'd leave the cabin and go over to his parents' cabin. Beau didn't blame her. Who would want to live with a snarly bear like him? He sure as hell wouldn't!

Beau felt tears stinging his eyes and forced them back. He cried too much already when he was alone, where no one could hear or see him. Supposing that his Delta Force training reinforced that men didn't cry, he didn't want to be found out. He was too ashamed of himself.

"Hey, son," Cletus said, casually leaning his broad shoulder against the opened door, "you doin' okay?"

Beau's Adam's apple bobbed once and he

looked away for a second and then turned, meeting his father's concerned blue gaze. "Yeah, Pa, I'm fine."

"You seem far away, like something's eating at ya, son. Want to tell me about it?"

"Just a lot on my mind, is all," Beau said. He didn't want to lie to his father because he'd taught him that honesty and truth were golden.

Cletus pushed his burly shoulder off the door jamb and came out, sitting down near Beau.

"Callie looks happy workin' with Ma," he said, gesturing in that direction.

"Yeah, she loves the earth, too."

"Just another reason to love her."

Nodding, Beau could feel his father's concern for him. Sometimes, he felt as if Cletus had radar capability or could actually read his mind. "Has she told you much about where she comes from? The Eagle Feather Ranch outside Butte, Montana?"

"Oh, not too much. Your ma, now, knows everything under the sun about your woman." He smiled a little, smoothing some of his mustache away from his upper lip.

"They get along well," Beau said, grateful. How badly he wanted to talk to his father about so many things, but he was afraid to.

"Indeed they do. They're like twins, almost. Your ma is a part of the land and so is Callie. That's a good thing."

Beau nodded, saying nothing, watching the women going up and down another long row they'd just weeded. "When you were in the Army . . ." he cocked his head, catching his father's gaze.

"Yes?"

"You said you were in the motor pool. Were you a driver?"

"I sure was. They didn't have any careers for me in woodworking or furniture making," he said, a chuckle rumbling out of his deep chest. He finished wiping his hands and added, "I was good with my hands and the Army in all its wisdom gave me a job tinkering with truck engines."

Smiling absently, Beau watched his mother in her bright red calico skirt that hung to her ankles, the colorful fabric swirling in and around her legs as she leaned over the row between them. Callie was in the next row, dressed in a pair of khaki twill capris, hitched up toward her knees as she began pulling weeds from the rich, black soil. "You're good with anything you touch, Pa."

"Rightly so, son. But my four years in the Army was tame compared with what you, Coy, and Jackson are doin'. I never got shot at. I was never overseas. So it was different from what you boys are having to deal with."

"You served your country, Pa. That's something to *always* be proud of," he said, holding his father's thoughtful gaze.

"That's true, son. But you boys are in black ops, something that I never was a part of. And something I don't have enough experience to understand."

Giving a soft snort, glad that there was no longer pain when he coughed, sneezed, or growled, Beau said, "And we can't tell you because it's all top secret."

His father's lips drew into a wry, twist. "They get you comin' and goin', Beau."

"What do you mean?"

"Well," Cletus said, gesturing toward the two women, "Callie told Ma about a week ago how you would wake up about four out of seven nights, yelling. It scared the bejesus out of her, of course. What was worse, according to Callie, was that she couldn't help you. She couldn't understand what you were going through to ask you the right questions. Ma pointed out to her that even if she did have the right questions, you couldn't answer them because you worked top secret and could tell no one, anything."

"Yeah," Beau muttered, shaking his head. "It's a gotcha for sure."

"Not just for Callie, though," he said gently, holding his son's stare, "but for us as well. Can you say anything to me about those nightmares that are waking you up screaming, son?"

Beau looked away, his gut in turmoil. "It's

just one nightmare, Pa. It replays the day I got shot."

"Humph," he rumbled. Frowning, he looked down at the ground in thought for a moment. "Is that something you can share with Callie?"

"I tried, but it was bloody. It's upsetting to her. I don't want to paint her a word picture of everything I went through. She's been through enough herself from that ambush. If I shared all of my nightmares, I think she'd start having nightmares again like she did at first when she got home. She's got PTSD just like me, Pa. And of late, those nightmares are becoming less and less frequent." He pushed his fingers in frustration through his short hair. "I'd just trigger more of those bad memories for her, Pa. That's not what I want to do."

"I hear you, son. And I don't disagree with you. We didn't know that Callie was having nightmares and PTSD." His dark brows fell and he studied the women for a moment. "You know, I think Callie is an awful lot like you, son. Only she doesn't have the excuse of having top secret information."

"What do you mean?"

"She tends to hide how she really feels and doesn't talk to anyone about it." Cletus gave him a knowing look. "Just like you three boys."

"But we can't talk about these things, Pa," he protested.

"That's all well and good for the Army. But in your case, it's hurtin' you, son. We all have to talk about what ails us to someone. Even if it's a tree or a rock." He pointed his bearded chin toward the women. "And Callie seems to be pretty closed up. She's not talkin' to anyone, either."

"Yes, that's a trait she has for sure," Beau said, scowling. "If it weren't for Graham McKinley, who was Marine black ops. He started pulling her out of it and got her to talk more to him than anyone else."

"Including you?"

"Yes, even me."

Scratching his head, Cletus rumbled, "From where I stand, you've got two clams who love one another and neither one of them knows how to open up and let the other one in. You don't know how to talk to one another, son."

Beau closed his eyes for a moment, pain ripping through his heart. Opening them, he rasped, "Pa, I've gotten some things out of Callie, but not a whole lot. I'm frustrated, not with her, but with myself. I guess I'm not asking the right questions or something. I don't know how to talk with her. I'm stymied."

Grunting, Cletus said, "It takes time for a man to learn how to talk to the woman he loves. Your ma and I had our ups and downs, for sure. She's emotional and it's the last place I want to be. For me, everything is black and white. It's like math: the answer is there if you just follow the common sense rules to find it." He smiled a little, watching Amber with a warm gaze. "All women are emotional, Beau. It's just who they are and I wouldn't change a hair on their heads. But it takes men a while to figure out what they're *really* saying, underneath the words."

"I've run into that with her, too. When she cries, I ache for her, Pa. I want to fix it. I want to do something to stop her from hurting, but I don't know how to do it."

"Oh," Cletus said, chuckling a little, "that one." He placed his hand on Beau's shoulder. "Tears for women are a release. They always feel better when they can let it all go. There's nothin' there for you to fix."

"Callie told me that."

His hand tightened a bit on Beau's shoulder. "And I taught all you boys that it's all right to cry. Better out than in, I say."

He knew his father was right. "I guess," he stumbled, his voice fraught with pain, "I feel like I'm staring at a big brick wall and there's no way over it or around it."

Patting his shoulder, Cletus said, "Then let Callie in, son. She's a lot stronger than you think she is. And even though she's still coming out of her own trauma from that ambush, she gets her strength from loving you. I've seen the heart give a person miles and miles of strength they didn't even realize they had until the vice grips were applied to 'em."

Lifting his hand off Beau's slumped shoulder, he added, "At hard times like these, let love be your compass, not your head. Don't let fear or pride ruin what you have with her. The more you both open up, the stronger you'll be together, in good times, and tough times. Just watch what happens, son. You'll be amazed."

CHAPTER 7

June 5

DESPITE HIS LACK of interest in food, Beau forced himself to eat his dinner that night in their small cabin. Callie had gone out of her way to make him a special dinner of beef pot roast with mashed potatoes, to get him to regain the twenty pounds he'd lost. He was now mobile and no longer having chest pain. His stomach was tight with anxiety and he didn't taste the food.

She had come in and showered earlier after being out in the garden half the day. Now, at the dinner table, her red hair was up in a loose knot on top of her head, looking beautiful with those half curled strands brushing her sunburned cheekbones. She smelled of fresh lemon and he knew Amber had given her a bar of the hand-made soap she'd made out of citrus flavors.

"Your nose is as red as your hair, Callie," he

teased, watching her eat hungrily at his left elbow.

"Oh, I know. Amber told me to wear a hat, but I didn't listen," she laughed, shaking her head. She poured some gravy into the mashed potatoes on her plate. "Next time, I'll borrow one of her straw hats."

"You look pretty," he said, watching her green eyes grow soft.

"Thanks," she whispered. "I saw you and your father out by his furniture barn. What were you talking about?"

He pushed the roast beef around on his plate, "Nothing much." His throat tightened.

"I'm so glad you have such a wonderful relationship with him."

"Do you miss your parents and grandparents?" She'd been with him at his home for a couple of months now. Beau had to think she was homesick or becoming so.

Callie frowned and then said, "I do and I don't. This time of year, everyone is gearing up to ride miles and miles of fence line to repair what was destroyed or weakened during the winter after the snows have melted. I would look forward to riding the fence line, but I hate handling barbed wire even with thick elk hide gloves on. I always got cut by it sooner or later, so no, I don't miss this part of the summer duties."

He looked toward the living room. "How are

you coming along on that blue afghan of yours."

"I like working on it at night when I'm tired. It's relaxing to sit and knit and watch TV with you."

"You really aren't homesick?"

"Sometimes," she admitted, using half of a fresh homemade biscuit to soak up the last of the gravy on her plate. "But getting to talk to everyone at home on Skype every week helps a lot."

He pushed the half-eaten plate of food away from him. "I'm sorry, I'm not hungry, Callie. I know you worked hard to make this great meal for us tonight."

Giving him a worried look, she said, "Don't worry about it. I'll put it in containers and we'll keep it for lunch tomorrow."

Nothing was ever wasted around here. Beau held her wide green eyes. "Do you think you'd be happier if you were home, Callie, instead of having to stay here and take care of me?"

Instantly, her thin red brows plummeted. Her lips pursed. She gave him a level, assessing look. "What kind of question is that, Beau?"

Hearing the edge in her smoky voice, he said, "I try to put myself in your shoes. If I was gone for months, I'd be pining for home, that's all."

Her scowl grew as she studied him. "There's more to that question than you're letting on. What's really bothering you, Beau?"

Hearing the frustration in her tone, he knew he could never lie to her. Not ever. "I'm waking you up every other night. You lose a lot of sleep because of my flashbacks and nightmares. I see the shadows under your eyes. I worry for you, Callie. I wonder if going home might be a vacation of sorts for you."

She snorted and her eyes flashed. "In your dreams, Gardner." Jabbing her finger down at the table, she bit out, "I don't want to be anywhere else but here, with you."

"You'd get more sleep." Desperation wound through him. This wasn't going the way he wanted. The anger leaped to her eyes and he felt it.

"Okay," she said roughly, pushing the chair back and standing up, "what's *really* going on here? What aren't you saying to me?"

Beau swallowed hard, seeing the fear and anxiety in her eyes. Dammit! He wasn't dealing with this well at all. "Don't be angry, Callie. Please? Sit down," he gestured to the chair behind her. "I'm not saying things well. I guess I'm not used to revealing my soul."

Her mouth twitched and she grabbed the chair, sitting down, and squaring off with him. "I get it, Beau. I really do. You may be black ops but you cannot hide behind that with me! That's not going to work." Her voice became tight with emotions. "I love you! That means you have to come clean with me. I'll deal with whatever you tell me, but don't keep hiding stuff from me. God, for the last month I've felt you building this wall between us. It's scared the hell out of me. I wonder if I'm doing it, or if I'm causing it by something I'm doing wrong." She looked away, a sheen of tears in her eyes, her mouth tight, trying to fight them back.

"No . . . it's nothing like that, Callie. It isn't. I love you, too. You've *got* to know that."

"How? When you close up and go away from me, Beau? When you hide? Do you know how that makes me feel?" She punched her thumb into her chest. "I feel like you're leaving me. Like I'm making you run away from me, but I don't know what I've done wrong. It's driving me crazy!"

Jesus! He stared at her, his mouth open, seeing the anguish in her eyes, hearing the hurt in her low, husky voice. Stumbling, he said, "You are not chasing me away, Callie."

"Well, then," she said, pain in her tone, "you won't kiss me. We haven't made love since you arrived here. I know at first you couldn't. But the doctor has said your lung injury is healed. I so badly want to sleep at your side again, Beau. I felt if I could, those nightmares might go away. I don't know what's going on inside you. I can't get into your head."

Crumpling inward, Beau was at a loss for

words. He felt those walls around himself, and wanted to hide behind them, avoiding Callie's concerns. "You've got this all wrong," he began. "Whatever is going on is with me, Callie, not you. Stop blaming yourself for this, will you?"

"Well, hell! If you won't communicate with me, Beau, what am I to think? Really! What am I to think about you? About us?" Her voice grew hoarse.

Beau didn't want her to cry. He just didn't. Opening his hands, he said, "I'm trying, Callie. But it's hard. I'm not used to spilling my guts about how I really feel."

"Like that's an excuse, Beau? Not in my world." She angrily took a swipe at her eyes. "I wonder if you really love me."

It felt as if another bullet had slammed into him. Frozen by her blurted words, all he could do was feel pain roaring through him, nonstop. "No . . .," he rasped, "no . . . that's not true at all, Callie. I DO love you!" Feeling as if his whole world had suddenly shattered, Beau winced as he saw tears spill out of her eyes, seeing the anger and hurt in them. "This is coming out all wrong," he said swiftly, holding up his hands.

She stared at him, her lower lip trembling until she compressed them. "I'm going for a walk. I need to clear my head."

She got up to leave, a devastated expression on her face. Then, she marched out and firmly closed the door to the cabin. She was gone.

That went well, didn't it?

He sat there, hands clasped on the table, staring into nothingness, his emotions churning and filled with frustration. His mind raced and he kept going over their heated, defensive conversation with one another. Callie had taken everything he said the wrong way, but he didn't blame her. He blamed himself. Women talked on several levels. His best friend, Matt Culver, and he had often commented that women were like a bunch of bus stations at a thousand different stops. They could easily hop from one station to another in a split second. And men, Matt had said, were like communication satellites circling Earth. They knew where they were and talked from one satellite to another, in a linear order. They didn't hop around from one satellite to another across the planet.

Wearily, he rubbed his face, trying to sort out why their talk had gone spinning out of control. He'd wanted to make sure Callie was okay staying with him. Was it getting to be too much of a burden on her shoulders? Beau knew she was still working through her active PTSD. Things like that did not just go away overnight, or even in a few months. It took years. *Years . . .*

Resting his jaw against his clasped hands, he closed his eyes, trying to sort through everything. It wounded him to think that Callie thought he didn't want to make love to her. And then, he had a bolt of insight. They were both laboring beneath the burden of PTSD. Both had nearly died. Callie's daily struggle to deal with her own near-death experience was no less intense than his was for him.

Opening his eyes, he cursed softly beneath his breath and pushed the chair away, rising. That was the key—well, one of them. The other was learning how to talk "women speak" with her, a subject in which he had no training.

Would Callie give him a chance, despite him bungling their dinnertime conversation? Pacing the cabin, he wondered where she was now. Beau knew she loved to walk the trails through the woodlands around the property. She also loved the barn, where she had made friends with the ewes that provided his ma with wool.

The June dusk was deep as he left the cabin, walking across the huge gravel area between all the buildings and the garden. He saw a light inside the barn, and figured Callie was inside. Sure enough, as he opened the door, he saw Callie over at the feed trough, petting all six of the ewes, which adored human attention. They were spoiled rotten by his ma, and they were gentle beings, but Beau had always loved all animals. He saw Callie lift her head and twist around. When she saw him, she frowned. He halted.

"I wanted to come and talk with you, Callie." Her hesitant look unsettled him, but he also saw her need for him in her eyes. Opening his hands, he said, "I need to sit and talk with you. We need to try and hash this out and make sense of it all, sweetheart."

The moment he'd spoken the endearment, Callie's whole face changed and he saw her raw love for him. Heartened, he stepped forward. Right now, Beau would rather face a firefight than try to unwind the snarled ball of emotions between them.

Sitting down on the wooden bench in front of the feed trough that was now empty, he gave her a hopeful look.

"I'm sorry I left like that," Callie admitted quietly. "That was childish. You deserve better from me."

Beau reached for her hand in her lap, curving his fingers around hers, giving her a long look, seeing the uncertainty in her gaze. "I screwed things up royally with you back in the cabin and I'm sorry too, Callie." He saw her face sag with so many emotions. "I need your help," he began, earnestly holding her gaze. "I don't know how to talk to a woman. It's not an excuse. I need you to teach me how to stay on whatever topic we start to talk about. Could you do that for me?"

Gulping, Callie nodded. "I get flustered, Beau, and I sometimes blow things out of proportion, like I did tonight."

"No, you didn't." He cupped her hand between his, turning it over, sliding his thumb lightly across her palm, feeling her react. "Here's what I see and you tell me if I'm on the money or not?"

"Go ahead . . ."

"First, we both have PTSD. We both had a life-and-death experience. That's what is beneath the surface, fueling us, and making us feel unbalanced."

"Yes, I think you're right."

Heartened, he added, "It's like an animal that lives in us, Callie. And sometimes it awakens me and I get these God-awful nightmares or flashbacks."

"And mine makes me irritable, short tempered, and then I feel defensive and threatened," Callie said, nodding.

"It attacks us differently, but we both get clawed, and we take it out on others around us whether we want to or not."

"Yes . . . you're right. I got angry at you, Beau."

"Rightfully so," he sighed. "I never expected you to ask me if I loved you or not." He touched the engagement ring on her left hand. "It caught me off guard, stunned me, I guess."

Wincing, Callie whispered, "I shouldn't have asked that, Beau. I didn't mean it the way it came out."

"It's okay. I think I've figured it out, but you let me know." She bobbed her head, and he could see her holding back a lot of feelings. Moving his thumb across each of her fingers, he rasped, "After I got the okay from the doc that I was ready for normal experiences, I didn't ask you to go to bed with me. You took it the wrong way and I don't blame you. Callie, I was afraid if I asked you back to bed with me, with all my tossing and turning, you'd *never* get any sleep. I was trying to protect you from me," he said, holding her luminous gaze. "I knew you were struggling too. I knew you needed your sleep. But you saw it as me pushing you away, didn't you?"

"Yes, I did. And I didn't understand why, Beau. You never told me any of this, so what was I to think?"

"I was afraid to tell you, Callie." It took everything he had to admit that to her.

"Why? I love you, Beau. My God, we've gone through so much together already."

Shaking his head, he muttered, "How about the monster called 'male ego?' Or the other one called 'pride?' I was afraid you'd see me as weak, less than the man you fell in love with." He released her hand. "What it comes down to is that I love you, whatever happens, forever. Never ever doubt that again. I'm sorry I've messed up with you, Callie. I don't mean to, but I'm going through my own hell and everything is distorted. I'm the one not thinking clearly right now. I remember back in November, in that ER at Bagram, when you sat there on the gurney after we were rescued. You looked wild-eyed, like a hunted, captured animal. I stood there feeling helpless, not knowing what to do or say. I wanted to hold you, but I was afraid to, because I thought you might have been raped."

"It was a terrible time for both of us," Callie choked. "You were standing guard over me and you'd been shot in the leg." She reached out, caressing his stubbled jaw. "Beau, I feel we have to give each other space and room. And I agree, our PTSD pattern is playing hell on us emotionally, as well as, mentally. It's not easy. Nothing is right now, for either of us."

Giving her a searching look, he asked, "What do you want to do about it?" He'd said the words heavily, slowly, because he was afraid Callie would walk out on him and leave him forever. Another part of his mind said that was foolish, he knew that Callie loved him and would be fiercely loyal to him until her last breath. He'd seen it in Afghanistan as they ran for their lives for days and nights. Never once had she whined, quit, or even asked to quit. No, Callie had gumption. She gave, and gave, and gave, until she had nothing more to give.

"I want to stay with you, Beau. I want to

sleep at your side. I don't care how many times a night you wake me up. I have a feeling if you'll let me stay with you, you won't have as many nightmares. I could be wrong," she said, shrugging, "but I'm lonely for you."

Her words melted his heart and fed his soul. "Okay, we'll do that. I want it, too. Now, as to the fact that I haven't made a move to love you . . ."

Callie grimaced. "Yes?"

"I was afraid," Beau said. "My head is wrapped up in anxiety all the time, Callie. In a good moment, I feel like my old self before this lung wound happened. Now, I'm always questioning myself, wondering if I can perform or not." He looked away.

"Okay, then let's take it a step at a time," Callie began. "You can touch me, kiss me, hold me when you want. You can also tell me when you don't feel like making love. At least then, I won't take it personally. I'll understand that the PTSD has a hold of you. There are times when I'm so wrapped up in anxiety, Beau, the last thing on my mind is sex. We can deal with that if we let each other know what's going on inside our heads."

"Does it strike you like that?"

"No, it's different for me, Beau. I have high anxiety buzzing around me 24/7. I'm getting so I know when the cortisol is screwing me over, so I wait to make decisions or statements after it lets me go. At first, when we brought you home, I accepted your wall as just that: anxiety that had you in its grip."

"No, I don't get much anxiety. But I get irritable and hot-tempered. I'm not normally that kind of person, Callie."

"No, you're easygoing and laid back."

"I hate this PTSD," he muttered.

"I'll join you on that one. At least we have one thing in our favor, Beau."

"What's that?"

"We have a common enemy: PTSD. We understand it because we live with it. Once we can straighten out our communication with one another, it should become an advantage. If you're getting crabby, I'll understand. If I'm getting impatient, I know you'll give me space."

Giving her a thoughtful glance, he said, "I hadn't looked at it in that way, but you're right."

"We have to devise keywords, or a sign of some kind to let the other know what's happening inside us. That can prevent a lot of misunderstanding."

Nodding, he murmured, "That sounds logical."

"We're in a new world, Beau. Nothing is what it was before these things happened to us." She grimaced. "We've changed, forever. But that doesn't mean our lives are over. Once we adjust over time, we'll get back on track with one another."

"I hate taking sleeping pills and anti-anxiety meds," he admitted. "I won't do it, right or wrong."

"I won't take them either. I feel like I'm half-alive when I do. That's not the quality of life I want." She sighed. "I may have anxiety a lot, but at least I know when it spikes and what's going on. And I can tell you when it happens, so we can discuss sensitive issues later, when those spikes have gone down."

"Right." He gave her an appraising look. "You're a smart little fox. Earlier, after you left the cabin, I'd suddenly had a lightbulb go on in my head. I figured out that our normal pattern with each other had been altered by the PTSD. That helped me understand why we were talking past one another." He added apologetically, "Callie, I'm going to stumble and fall a lot with you on this talking bit. I know how important it is to communicate, but I honestly feel scared that I'll screw up so badly, you'll give up on me."

"That's not going to happen, Beau. We need a time-out word or gesture when we reach a point like we did back there in the cabin. We both have to take a step back and agree to discuss it at another time when we're not prisoners of our own anxiety and the high cortisol flooding our systems."

"I want to do this, but I'm feeling pretty shaky about it," Beau admitted. "It's not that I don't want to try it, Callie. I do."

"We're like two people without a skin to protect ourselves any longer, Beau. At least, that's the way I feel at times. And when we're horribly vulnerable, feeling like we're under threat, we need to tell one another, like you did with me just now. You told me how you really felt. You have no idea how refreshing that is to me. Now, I don't have to let my wild imagination take me to stupid scenarios that are untrue. At least now, I know you're feeling like you're on quicksand. I get that. I can handle that."

"But we're not always going to be perfect at this, Callie. We're human. I hope you don't set me up on a pedestal and think I'm not going to slip off it more times than not."

"I hope the same thing from you, Beau," she told him, reaching over, touching his hand. "I know how much patience you had with me before you got wounded."

"I still have that patience," he reassured her. Taking her hand, he kissed it. "I think our love will give us the tolerance we need so long as we talk honestly."

"I believe that," Callie said wistfully. She leaned forward, kissing him on the mouth.

Beau luxuriated in the softness of her lips skimming his. He closed his eyes, feeling her fingers wrap around his as he leaned toward her. She smelled so good! Her flesh was soft and fragrant. Already, he could feel his erection stirring. It was the first time that had happened since he'd been shot. As he eased from her wet lips, drowning in the luster of her half-open green eyes, he wondered if their talk had removed some of the burden he'd felt every day. The tension that had stiffened his shoulders was suddenly, miraculously gone, too.

"You're right," he rasped, lifting his other hand, smoothing some strands from her temple. "We're like raw meat thrown out on a hot sidewalk, left to burn on it."

She chuckled and sat up, continuing to hold his hand. "That sorta says it all. Quite a verbal visual you gave me, Gardner."

Perking up, loving her teasing of him, he gave her a bashful grin. "That's okay. We have one another, Callie. And that's all that counts. If I have to have this curse the rest of my life, I'm glad you're at my side. No other person could ever understand what we go through daily."

"And I sure wouldn't want to have to go through this with someone who didn't understand."

Some of the ewes crowded over to where she sat, straining their thick, short necks in the direction of her knees, wanting her touch, once more. She smiled and leaned over, dutifully scratching the top of each of their heads. "We have to start over with one another, Beau. We can't go back to how we were before. We're in a new world together. We're going to have to ask a lot of questions and both of us has to be willing to tell the truth. And that takes guts. Okay?"

"Okay," he said, watching each ewe close her eyes with satisfaction as Callie scratched each of their heads. He watched her for a moment, wanted her hands on him. An ache grew in his heart and he yearned to have her against his body, in their bed, naked, warm, and willing.

Mouth dry, he said, "Would you like to come to bed with me tonight, Callie? Lie at my side?" He saw her eyes fill with joy.

"I'd love that, Beau!"

"I can't promise you anything. I mean, I want to, but I'm scared as hell. I'm scared that PTSD will rear its ugly head."

"We'll talk through it," she said, her voice choked up. "Let's just take one step at a time."

A huge load slid off his shoulders. Studying her, he demanded, "Are you sure, Callie?" What if he couldn't get it up? That scared him more than anything else except for her walking out on him forever.

"What matters is that you hold me close, Beau. I need to lay my head on your good shoulder. That's all I need right now. It's more than enough for me."

CHAPTER 8

CALLIE FELT HOPE racing through her as she stood with Beau in the shower. It was too small to inspire much messing around, but she happily washed his back for him, kissed his nape, and when he turned around, he kissed her long, hard, and deeply. And that told her all she needed to know beneath the streams of warm water.

They laughed as they stepped out because they could barely turn around in the plastic enclosure without bumping into one of the walls. She towel-dried him, noticing the deep pink of his scar in the middle of his right side, across his ribcage. She pulled a towel across his broad shoulders, wanting to keep him warm because the June night was cool. The steam hung in the bathroom where they stood. "That looks so tender," she said, placing her fingers lightly across the scar.

"It is," he said, pulling the towel across her shoulders, gently patting her neck and shoulders dry.

"Does it hurt when you move?"

"Twisting a lot does hurt," he admitted. "But with time, the doc said it will stop hurting. I'm okay. Really," he said, cupping her face, leaning down, and sliding his mouth along hers. Naked, they closed the gap between them and held each other close.

Her nipples hardened even more as he kissed her slowly, his breath moist against her cheek. She moaned as she brushed herself against him, her whole body on fire as his mouth worshipped her. She eased her arms up and over his shoulders, pulling herself fully against him. Callie could feel Beau's erection—it had been there since they'd stepped into the shower together. Now, his hard length was pressing insistently into her belly, letting her know in another way how much he desired her. It felt so good! It had been such a long, harrowing road that they'd walked together since she'd seen him in Bethesda at the medical center.

Drowning in the strength and tenderness of his mouth, Callie wanted nothing more than to be with Beau in every possible way. Her thoughts began to dissolve as his hands left her face and drifted downward, cupping her lush breasts. He stepped back so he could brush her nipples with his thumb, and her knees nearly caved from the electricity leaping between them. His erection became even harder, if that was possible. She heard him groan as he stroked her breasts with his large, calloused hands. Sparks of fire erupted in every cell of her body from the pleasure. Already, she was damp between her legs, this time not with water, but with her own fluids, as her body responded to his tender ministrations.

"I want you," Beau said raggedly against her wet lips. "Tell me what you want, Callie," and he drew back just far enough to look into her eyes, awash with a hungry desire for him.

"Let's go to bed," she said, her voice tremulous, heavy with need for him.

They quickly dried off, holding hands as they walked into their small bedroom. Night had fallen, a full moon rising in the east, sending slats of milky light through one of the two windows. Callie pulled down the covers on her side of the squeaky, old brass bed that had stood the test of decades in the log home. She grinned as she climbed in.

"It could get noisy in here, Beau."

He returned her wicked look. "That's okay by me." He got into bed, pushing the sheet and blankets to the footboard. "Okay with you?"

Callie watched him lie down on his back. "Fine by me." She knelt near his left side, placing her hand lightly across his thick erection. "Tell me how we go about this. I know your right side is still tender and healing. What's the best position, Beau?" Beau had been hurt enough. Callie didn't want to cause him more pain. All she wanted was to kiss this man senseless, and have him plunge deep inside her and be one with her.

"I don't know," he said, hesitantly. "We've not made love with one another since I got hit."

She watched his eyes shutter close as she wrapped her fingers teasingly around him. He arched into her hand, groaning, gripping her hand, holding her in place. "Feel good?"

"You know it does," he managed. "Don't stop."

And she didn't. Her mind raced over possible positions with Beau and each one seemed to put pressure on his ribcage. She slowly kneaded his erection, hearing him groan with pleasure, and she leaned over, kissing him.

Instantly, Beau slid his hand across her nape, her thick hair falling around them as she searched his mouth. Everything felt so good, so natural, and her heart's doors flew open with joy as she hungrily met his tongue with hers. Breathing shallowly, she pulled from his mouth, keeping her hand around him, staring into his narrowed, glittering eyes as he studied hers.

He was now the hunter and she, his prey. It was exciting to feel him stalking her like this. She reveled in his masculinity, giving herself completely to him in every way.

"Tell you what," she whispered, kissing the corners of his mouth, "I think the best position is for me to be on my hands and knees, and you can come from behind me."

"I was thinking the same thing," he admitted. "Are you okay with it?"

She gave him a grin. "Am I? Oh, yes!" She stopped short of telling him that he gave her wonderful orgasms in that position because she didn't want to put undue pressure on Beau to perform. Even if he could come and she didn't have any orgasms, Callie was fine with it. He was still healing. Judging from his erection, however, she was sure Beau could perform, but she wasn't about to mention it.

"All I want," she whispered against his mouth, "is for us to celebrate the fact that we love one another, Beau. Nothing more. Just getting to touch you again, to kiss you, is enough for me." There was an instant look of relief in his eyes and she thanked her woman's intuition for knowing ahead of time that he was worried about pleasing her. "Let's just touch, kiss, and feel our bodies together again. No expectations."

She leaned down, placing small, wet kisses along his jaw, his corded neck, and then, across his chest. She nibbled on his nipples and his hips bucked into her hand that was still holding his erection. Smiling to herself, Callie silently promised the man she loved that she would leave no square inch of him untouched tonight. This was a celebration after making it through the darkness, coming into the light, albeit slowly and with trepidation. She knew both of them felt anxious about pleasing the other as completely as they had before his wounding.

By the time she moved to her hands and knees, Beau was more than ready to come. As he pressed his erection against her wet opening, Callie braced, his hands tightening around her hips, pressing forward. She wasn't sure who groaned more loudly when he sheathed slowly into her. The sensations were delicious, stretching and widening her, making her shake with the need for an orgasm.

Leaning back against him, she sucked him more deeply into her tight confines. His fingers dug into her flesh, alive with the pleasure she knew she was giving him. Callie wouldn't allow him to pull out of her; she kept easing back against his body, asking him to thrust repeatedly into her.

She knew that Beau needed this, needed to come inside her. Being able to cement their relationship on a new level, a different one, was her priority. Love had many dimensions and she loved Beau enough to sacrifice herself for him, to strengthen his belief that as a man, he was as potent a lover, and a man, as he had been before.

And once he began to slowly thrust into her, hearing his groan of utter ecstasy, she felt her love grow even more powerful. With each pumping motion, her own body heated up, leaped to life as he surged into her, orgasmic fire erupting within her. She cried out, her fingers digging deeply into the mattress beneath her hands, hurled into an inner space of utter release and satisfaction. And then, she heard him growl, freeze, feeling him release deep within her.

Callie sobbed with joy and relief. As she felt Beau collapse and lie across her back, his head resting against hers in the aftermath, she was grateful. Whatever those blockades and walls erected by the PTSD, they seemed to collapse with each climax. It was a new piece of information for her as she swam in the heated pool of their wet, sated bodies clinging together as they absorbed each other. Callie, luxuriated in his arms, gently wrapping herself around him. Beau kissed her hair, nape, and her damp cheek.

Still gasping from the pleasure moving in undulating ripples throughout her lower body, she hungrily absorbed Beau's strength and masculinity. Finally, he gently eased out of her, turned her over, and guided her to lie down on her right side, her body resting against his. Their breathing was heavy as they lay together. She nestled her head against his left shoulder, desperately needing his arm around her, his fingers stroking slowly up and down her damp back. Callie was a satisfied woman, fulfilled at last, as she nuzzled into his neck and jaw, wanting nothing more.

BEAU FELT CALLIE'S lush body against his as he slowly emerged from his deep, healing sleep. She was much smaller than he was, but felt like a cushiony pillow against his long, hard, lean body. His arm was beneath her neck, and hers was curved around his waist, away from his wound. Just the citrus scent on her skin, the silkiness of her hair against his jaw, made him smile. He was in heaven, or as close as he was ever going to get to it, here on Earth. This woman made his heart fill with such love that it left him speechless. The gentle warmth in his chest spread like a soft breeze throughout him. He heard the sounds of nature outside their windows, saw the morning light spilling in, illuminating the small, simple room.

Rolling his head to the left, he placed a soft kiss on Callie's hair. She fit him like a glove and he relished the feeling of her against him once again. The months without her beside him had torn him apart and made him question his own masculinity, and whether he would be able to please her again. As he lay there, eyes closed, his arms around her, holding her close. He remembered their meeting, her electrifying belly dance at that chow hall where the Thanksgiving USO show was being held.

Looking back on that time, he knew that he'd immediately fallen for the redhead whose green eyes flashed with such life. That purple and silver belly dancing outfit made her that much more beautiful to him. Her grace was that of a ballerina. Only it wasn't ballet. It was primal, teasing belly dancing at its finest.

He'd fallen so hard for Callie that he'd pursued her until he caught her. It hadn't been easy. In fact, it had been rocky as hell, but Beau had persevered because he knew deep in his heart that this was the woman he wanted to spend the rest of his life with. This was the woman he wanted to marry, the one who would carry his children.

Only now they had PTSD, a new layer weighing down on them, and on their relationship. But Beau didn't care. He had enough belief in them to transcend it. They might have to live with it the rest of their lives, but they'd learn how to direct it, and not allow it to tear them apart. The hormone released by PTSD, cortisol, kept them in a constant, heightened state of anxiety, surging into a fight-or-flight reflex when least expected.

He sighed, sliding his fingers slowly up and

down her curved spine. Her flesh was warm and firm. Callie was in top athletic condition because of the belly dancing exercises she did every day without fail. And last night, hey, he'd given her an orgasm. Never had he been so relieved, so grateful, as at that moment.

Beau hadn't wanted to let Callie know how much he was questioning his ability to please her. What if he couldn't? But all his worries dissolved after her orgasm. Yes, he still had it in him. He could still please her. Yes!

Callie stirred, making soft, snuffling sounds as she began to awaken. Beau smiled and opened his eyes, wanting to see her eyelashes drift open. He eased her a little downward on his arm so he could watch her awaken. Those crimson strands of hair were thick, wild, and tousled, just like her. He was so glad she was a lover of nature, of the land. He couldn't see himself marrying some city slicker.

She lifted her long, graceful fingers, rubbing her nose, and then her sleepy looking eyes. Those thick, red lashes against her flushed cheeks brought out a dappling of freckles across them and her nose. But it was her sculpted lips that stirred his heart and once more, his erection. He was surprised, but then thought, *Why not?* She was a sensual woman in every way and he appreciated her on so many levels from physical, to emotional, and mental. She appealed to him in every possible way.

"You're beautiful when you wake up," he told her in a husky voice, caressing her cheek, moving his thumb across her warm skin.

"Ummm, I feel groggy, but great," she muttered.

"It was great. More than great. It isn't like we haven't been under a gun," he told her, giving her an apologetic look for the pun.

"I think it was that wonderful orgasm that symbolized that we're now going to be in an up cycle with one another," she whispered, leaning up to give him a quick kiss on the mouth. "That felt so good."

Inwardly, Beau preened over her comments. "I always want to please you. Always."

Callie slowly sat up, stretching her arms over her head. "You have *always* pleased me, Beau. We might be changed in some ways, but not in all ways. I'm going to get up and make us coffee. Want to join me out in the kitchen?"

"Sure," he murmured, pulling the covers pooling around her hips aside. "I'm gonna get a shower first." He took in her naked body, those full, firm breasts, those hard nipples just begging to be suckled by him once more. Beau resisted. He was sure Callie would be sore from last night's session with one another. When she moved, she was all grace, curves, and beauty. Mentally taking a picture of Callie, he wanted to remember this moment forever, because it was the first day of their new lives together.

June 21

"HOW DO YOU think your parents will feel about you leaving here and coming back to the ranch with me?" Callie asked Beau over lunch on a bench outside their cabin. The day was unusually warm, and all the trees had sprouted green leaves for the summer. She had made them tuna sandwiches, added potato chips, and they'd sat against the cabin wall on a bench his father had made decades earlier.

"They know I'm going home to the ranch with you, Callie," he said between bites. "Your grandfather offered to teach me how to become a foreman, and run the ranch a decade from now. I know your grandparents want to retire and Graham said it would take about ten years to turn me from a hill boy into a cowboy." He grinned, giving her a merry look. "And your dad never wanted to run the ranch, so it's a good fit for me to step in and get trained."

Callie nodded, munching on the sliced sweet pickles she'd placed on another plate between them. "No, my dad loves our ranch, but he has his own career. And I know he's grateful that you'll be carrying it on for the family. I feel bad taking you from your mom and dad, though," she admitted. "I love Amber and Cletus. They're salt of the earth people, like you, Beau."

"It does run in our family," Beau said with a chuckle. "A hill person can live anywhere in the world, but they'll never lose that hill blood. I won't lose that part of myself if I trade my baseball cap in for a cowboy hat."

"I don't want you changed. I love you just the way you are, Beau."

"I know. But I gave Graham my word that I'd take care of you, Callie."

She studied him for a moment, wiping her fingers off with a paper napkin. "Would you rather stay here, Beau?"

"Nah. I'm not a woodworker, Callie. There's no job for me here on Black Mountain. And I sure don't want some clerking job in Dunmore. I'd never make enough money to give us a decent life. There's no call for black ops guys like me, except in security businesses, and I don't want to do that anymore."

"I like you as a cowboy."

"So do I. It's hard, outdoor work, but I'm accustomed to that, Callie. I like being outside and in the elements." He finished off his sandwich, wiping his mouth with the napkin. "I like that life is going to happen for us together."

"We'll weather whatever comes our way, Beau. PTSD or not."

"Yes, we'll do that together." He offered her

the last sweet pickle and she shook her head.

"I called my parents last night," Callie offered. "I told them we booked airline tickets and gave them our arrival time at the Butte airport tomorrow afternoon."

"Good. I imagine they were glad to hear you're coming home."

"Actually, they were glad *we* were coming home. I got to talk to Grandpa, and he's picked out a nice quarter horse for you, a buckskin named Frank. He said he's an older, wiser horse, and will be perfect for you while you learn how to ride."

Smiling, Beau said, "He's always had my back and I appreciate that."

Callie stacked the plates between them. The sunlight felt wonderful and she relished in the warmth from it. "When we get home, I'm going to start learning accounting from Mom. I've always had a good head for numbers and I know that when my grandparents retire, my parents will want me to pitch in. I'm good at details, math, and such. I told her last night that I'd go into training with her so I can understand the business end of the ranch for when you and I take it over."

"Everything changes, doesn't it?"

"Grandpa's favorite saying is, 'The only thing we can count on is change.'"

Beau turned, slipping her left hand into his.

"And there's one change that I'm looking forward to . . ." holding her gaze he said, "marrying you."

"Same here," Callie whispered, suddenly emotional. Wrapping her fingers around his, she said, "My mom and grandma want to know if we've set a date yet."

"What do you think? I'm open, Callie, to whatever you want."

"How about this fall? Maybe early September? And could your parents come visit us at the ranch, then?"

"We can talk to them tonight about it. Ma is making us a special going-away dinner tonight. I think they'd both come, but my pa always has orders for his furniture to be done at specific times."

Nodding, Callie said, "Well, let's find out, because I want them at the ranch for the wedding, Beau. I know my family will love them just as I do." She gave him a warm look, "I think they'll all become great, wonderful friends."

"I'm sure that the Thorn family would come off the top of Black Mountain to feed all our critters here and take care of them while they're away. That's what we do for each other here."

"Good, because I know your father refuses to fly. He'll have drive up to Montana."

Chuckling, Beau nodded. "Yeah, Pa was in an airplane accident when he was in Army. They were flying a bunch of motor pool mechanics to another area and was one of the few to walk away from it. He swore then to never step foot in another plane again, and he hasn't."

She slid her hand across his jaw. "Let's see what his schedule is like for furniture delivery in September, then. We can change the date if there's a conflict. Okay?"

"I know he'd appreciate that."

She gazed into his clear gray eyes, seeing the happiness in them. Callie smiled and nodded. "I love your parents. I love you."

"I'm relieved we're talking with one another, Callie."

The rough patch was their PTSD. Callie knew that there was no cure for it. Only moderating or turning down the volume on the symptoms. Although, over time, some vets had found that some of their symptoms began to wane. Maybe theirs would too? She didn't know. It was something they just had to live with. "Yes, we'll keep at it," she said softly.

"We'll keep working at it, though," he agreed. Giving her a boyish look, he added, "You're teaching me a whole new level of communication: 'Women Speak 101.'"

Laughing, Callie understood. Men thought one way, women thought another. But that didn't mean they couldn't find ways to hear one another, or to listen closely to what the other was saying. In the weeks since their argument, they'd both sat down to really listen to one another. And the truth be known, Callie was just as much at fault for her assumptions as Beau was. Now, they were trying their best to break the translation barrier that stood between them. And it was working.

"Well, as you put it, 'Male Speak 101' is just as entangled for me. I'm not a linear thinker like you, Beau. I never will be, but at least I understand where you're coming from and that's a huge help."

Snickering, he slid his fingers through her hair, moving it away from her temple. "I sure like the way we communicate in bed. How about you?"

Laughing, she drowned in his amused gray gaze. "Oh, no translation needed there!"

They laughed together and Beau leaned over, kissing her warmly and lingeringly. Callie eagerly leaned forward, wanting more closeness. Beau was her life partner, as she was his. They had an equal partnership. They respected one another. And they'd gone so far as to have PTSD together as well. That she could have done without, but she knew from growing up on a Montana ranch, that not all of life was roses. It had thorns in it too. "Rough patches," as Beau referred to them.

They had a chapter in their lives coming to an end and a new chapter beginning back at the

Eagle Feather Ranch in Butte, Montana. She had no idea what would happen next, but Callie didn't care, because she knew that the man kissing her right now loved her with his life. Now and forever.

THE BEGINNING...

Don't miss Lindsay McKenna's
next DELOS series novella,

Unbound Pursuit

Available from Lindsay McKenna and Blue
Turtle Publishing and wherever you buy eBooks!

Turn the page for a sneak peek of
Unbound Pursuit!

Excerpt from

Unbound Pursuit

T AL CULVER HAD turned around to watch Mattie, who with swift, knowing precision had gone to work dumping the paint-filled water from the thirty jars, washing them, and turning them upside down to dry on tea towels she'd set on the countertop. The back door opened and closed, getting Tal's attention. The children could come and go through two different exits. The side door led to the playground. The rear door, near the sink where Mattie worked, was hidden from view by a large mudroom. The hair on the back of her neck rose, instantly making Tal focus her attention on the entrance.

What the hell? Normally that reaction served to warn her that there was danger nearby, and it wasn't something Tal ignored. She was in Texas in a kindergarten classroom. Why was she suddenly on high alert?

Mattie heard the door open and close, too. She barely looked up, busily washing out the Mason jars. She didn't want to be late getting Tal back to the ranch. Her mother was making a special meal of leg of lamb tonight for the family, and she needed to get home to help her with making the salad and the mashed potatoes and gravy. She figured it was the parent of a child who had forgotten something in the classroom coming back to pick it up.

A dark shape appeared at the entrance. Mattie turned. She gasped. The Mason jar in her hand slipped and fell to the floor, shattering.

"Mark!" The word came flying out of her mouth. Mattie's heart pounded in her chest as she stared up into his narrowed gold-brown eyes. He wore a black Stetson, a white long-sleeved shirt with a black leather vest over it, jeans, and cowboy boots. His mouth . . . oh, lordy, his mouth . . . she remembered only too well how wonderful he was at kissing her.

She took a step back, her eyes huge as she stared in disbelief at him. He stood motionless, like a tense statue. Mark's gaze shot to Tal and then back to her.

"Who's this with you, Mattie?"

She hadn't heard his voice in nearly three months, that same low, sensual drawl of his that made her melt, made her lower body burn with need of him. Gulping, she jerked a look toward Tal. "That's Tal, my friend," she managed to say, choked up. She turned toward him. "What are you doing here?" Tears clogged her eyes but

Mattie refused to let them fall, straightening her spine, throwing back her shoulders, her chin jutting out, anger flowing through her along with her shock.

"I need to talk to you alone," Mark growled. "Get rid of her?"

Mattie scowled. Anger took over. "Go to hell, Mark!" She jabbed her finger toward the door of the mudroom. "Just get the hell out of my life! How dare you come back into it! You think you can just waltz in here after being gone three months without a word?" Her voice was shaking, she was so angry and hurt. And he looked so delicious to her. He was half Chippewa Indian through his mother, who was now dead. He had his mother's coppery skin, that shining short black hair, those glittering, intelligent wolf eyes, as she used to refer to them, a gold-brown mixture. His mouth thinned, relaxed a little. For a split second, Mattie thought he'd smiled, or that maybe some amusement had flittered across his narrowed, intelligent gaze.

"I've been real busy, Mattie. That's not the welcome I was hoping for."

Mattie gulped back her tears. "What the hell else did you expect?"

Mark shrugged lazily, lifting one shoulder, keeping his gaze pinned on Tal. The woman seemed like someone he wouldn't want to mess with. Mark saw the look in her eyes, saw the fine tension in her body, and felt the energy around her. If she wasn't law enforcement, then she was military. He met her gaze and hardened his look in her direction, willing her to stay right where she was. Missing nothing upon first perusal, Mark could quickly size up another person and know just how dangerous they were. This woman was damned dangerous, even though she wore a camel-colored pantsuit with a bright orange tee beneath it. She wore no makeup, her black hair lying like a shining cloak around her proud shoulders.

His gaze moved back to Mattie. "I need to talk to you," he repeated.

Snorting vehemently, she snapped, "I want *nothing* to do with you, Mark!"

His gut clenched, his heart twisting with guilt and need of her. Mark tried to bury the pain he carried deep within him. He watched the flare of righteous anger in Mattie's slitted dark green eyes. Reining in the desire for her that was always with him, he rasped, "Okay, then here it is: you tell your father to keep his wranglers out of the northeast corner of your ranch two nights from now, Mattie." His voice dropped. "This isn't a joke. You need to keep everyone out of that area." He started to turn, stopped himself, lifting his head, meeting Mattie's tear-filled eyes. Less gruffly, the hardness in his gold-brown eyes dissolving, almost turning tender, he said, "Take good care of yourself, Mattie . . ."

Before Mattie could snarl at him, he turned on his heel and was gone. When the door slammed shut, Mattie jumped. She was breathing raggedly, her heart sledgehammering in her chest. Gulping, she looked at Tal.

"Are you okay?" Mattie asked in a trembling tone.

Giving a slight nod, Tal said, "I'm fine. Is he gone?" She gestured with her chin toward where Mark had disappeared.

Turning, Mattie quickly walked out to the mudroom. Peering out the window, she saw nothing but the outskirts of Van Horn. It was as if Mark had never been there. But he had. She had goose bumps across her skin, and she absently rubbed her upper arms, feeling stunned by his sudden and unexpected presence.

She heard Tal get up, the chair scraping back against the tiled floor. Because of her ankle, she couldn't move quickly, and Mattie hurried back and met her at the sink. "He's gone."

"Did you see where he went?"

Shaking her head, she whispered, "No . . . I looked, but he's like a ghost. Just . . . gone." Touching her brow, she added apologetically, "I'm so sorry, Tal. You didn't need this. God, I didn't need it either."

Tal reached out, feeling her shaking. Mattie's face was white, her freckles standing out against her tightened skin. "How are you doing? Do you want to come and sit down? Can I get you a drink of water?" Tal could feel the tension in her, saw the tears glimmering in her eyes. Mattie was valiantly trying not to cry. "Come on," Tal urged her gently, "come and sit down for a minute." Mattie looked so shaken Tal wasn't sure she wasn't going to faint on her. And if she did, Tal wouldn't be able to break her fall, thanks to her weakened ankle.

Jerkily, Mattie nodded, covering her eyes for a moment, trying to hold herself together. She tried to shove down her dark past, her love for Mark. After all he'd done to her! If the towns-people ever knew what had happened, she'd never live it down. Never had she ever wanted anyone but Mark. It was a destiny and a curse. She still loved him. Mattie denied it, but inside, in her private moments, her heart ached for Mark.

Around her, from childhood onward, Mark had been vulnerable, despite his hard life. Mattie had seen the scars where his flesh had been peeled back when his angry, alcoholic father would unmercifully beat him with his belt. She knew he'd gotten those scars when he'd stepped between his father and his sister, Sage. Matt had made himself a target to protect Sage from being sexually molested. His body had been deeply scarred over time. To this day, Sage's loyalty to her brother was solid, and Mattie knew why.

Mark had protected her from her father. And Sage loved her brother as fiercely as Mattie did, but for different reasons.

Sitting down, Mattie was grateful for Tal's quiet strength, her hand resting on her slumped shoulder as she tried to control her inner tumult. "I don't know why he suddenly showed up," she whispered, her voice quavering. Tears spilled down her cheeks, and she turned her head, ashamed that Tal would see her cry.

"Did you know he was coming?"

"N-no," she whispered, quickly wiping the tears away, humiliated that her future sister-in-law-to-be was seeing her like this, a muddled mass of jellied emotions, pulverized by Mark's shocking appearance.

"Has he done this before?"

Shaking her head, Mattie said hoarsely, "I have not seen him in three months. I figured he'd just disappeared out of my life forever. That's why I was so shocked to see him again."

Frowning, Tal smoothed her hand gently across Mattie's shaking shoulders. She was crying. Tal put herself in Mattie's place. This would be a helluva shock for anyone to take. Almost like a dead person returning from the grave.

"I-I'm sorry, Tal. I shouldn't be crying. You'd think I'd learn my lesson . . ."

"Sometimes, when you love someone, it takes a long time to get over it," Tal told her.

"I-I shouldn't still love him!" she rasped, giving Tal a confused look. "How can I?"

"Only you can answer that," Tal said gently, smoothing back some strands of red hair that were sticking to her damp cheek. "Love and grief are entwined, I've found. And it's a process you work through. There's no time limit on it."

Sniffing, Mattie pulled a tissue out of her pocket, wiping her eyes and blowing her nose. "There's so much grief and sadness shared between us. I knew one day he'd leave for good. And I thought he had. But he's back . . . I-I never expected to ever see him again."

Never mind she still dreamed like the child she was of what might have been if they'd married once they were out of high school. The year they spent together when they were teenagers, after their relationship moved from friendship to something more, had been heaven on earth. Mark been so gentle and open with her, so incredibly loving. Sometimes, Mattie felt as if Mark had a lifetime of love stored up for her from the time he was born. At six years old, seeing him in the first grade, she'd fallen in love with him. It was the most beautiful feeling in the world to have him unveil the deepest, most beautiful parts of himself, his dreams, his wishes, with her. People called it puppy love, but the feeling had never gone away. And when she was sixteen and he finally opened up to her, let himself be as vulnerable as she was, and tenderly loved her, her soul had wept with joy and pleasure. He had been that loving. But then their lives had spiraled into a darkness she could never have imagined. And it had torn them apart even though they still ached to be with one another.

After that, Mark had changed abruptly. Forever. He was no longer open with her; he shut down. She knew why. It was a secret both of them would carry to their graves. The more Mattie tried to remain close to Mark, the more he retreated from her, those hard shields that he had always kept between himself and most other people began rising against her, too, cutting her off from his soft side. Mattie was too ashamed, too guilty and young, to figure out how to salvage the love they held for one another. And to this day, she beat herself up, knowing that one night had changed their lives and made Mark suddenly disconnect from her forever.

"We need to get home," Tal urged her quietly. "Your dad and Wyatt need to know what just happened. Can I help you get things straightened up around here so we can leave?"

Mattie gave a jerky nod, wiping her cheeks dry. "Y-yes, Dad and Wyatt need to know what happened," she whispered unsteadily, pushing the chair back. "You stay put, Tal. It will take me about ten minutes to get everything in order. I don't want you trying to run around on that bum ankle of yours."

The Books of Delos

Title: ***Last Chance*** (Prologue)
Publish Date: July 15, 2015
Learn more at:
delos.lindsaymckenna.com/last-chance

Title: ***Nowhere to Hide***
Publish Date: October 13, 2015
Learn more at:
delos.lindsaymckenna.com/nowhere-to-hide

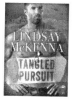

Title: ***Tangled Pursuit***
Publish Date: November 11, 2015
Learn more at:
delos.lindsaymckenna.com/tangled-pursuit

Title: ***Forged in Fire***
Publish Date: December 3, 2015
Learn more at:
delos.lindsaymckenna.com/forged-in-fire

Title: ***Broken Dreams***
Publish Date: January 2, 2016
Learn more at:
delos.lindsaymckenna.com/broken-dreams

Title: ***Blind Sided***
Publish Date: June 5, 2016
Learn more at:
delos.lindsaymckenna.com/blind-sided

Title: ***Secret Dream***
Publish Date: July 25, 2016
Learn more at:
delos.lindsaymckenna.com/secret-dream

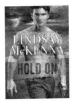

Title: ***Hold On***
Publish Date: August 3, 2016
Learn more at:
delos.lindsaymckenna.com/hold-on

Everything Delos!

Newsletter

Please sign up for my free quarterly newsletter on the front page of my official Lindsay McKenna website at lindsaymckenna.com. The newsletter will have exclusive information about my books, publishing schedule, giveaways, exclusive cover peeks, and more.

Delos Series Website

Be sure to drop by the website dedicated to the Delos series at delos.lindsaymckenna.com. There will be new articles on characters, publishing schedule and information about each book written by Lindsay.

Quote Books

I love how the Internet has evolved. I had great fun create "quote books with text" which reminded me of an old fashioned comic book . . . lots of great color photos and a little text, which forms a "book" that tells you, the reader, a story. Let me know if you like these quote books because I think it's a great way to add extra enjoyment with this series! Just go to my Delos Series website delos. lindsaymckenna.com, which features the books in the series.

The individual downloadable quote books are located on the corresponding book pages. Please share with your reader friends!

34882078R00104

Made in the USA
Middletown, DE
08 September 2016